SILHOUETTE DESIRE IS PROUD
TO PRESENT A BRAND-NEW MINISERIES
BY BESTSELLING AUTHOR
LEANNE BANKS

A millionaire…a bad boy…a protector.

Three strong, sexy men take on the ultimate
challenge: love!

9/98: Millionaire Dad
10/98: The Lone Rider Takes a Bride
11/98: Thirty-Day Fiancé

This month, meet Rulebreaker Joe Caruthers—
a handsome millionaire who unexpectedly
becomes a father….

Don't miss any of these Silhouette Desire novels!

Dear Reader,

This month, Silhouette Desire is celebrating milestones, miniseries—and, of course, sensual, emotional and compelling love stories. Every book is a treasured keeper in Lass Small's miniseries THE KEEPERS OF TEXAS, but this month, the continuation of this wonderful series about the Keeper family marks a milestone for Lass—the publication of her 50th book for Silhouette with *The Lone Texan,* also our MAN OF THE MONTH selection!

Desire is also proud to present the launch of two brand-new miniseries. First, let us introduce you to THE RULEBREAKERS, Leanne Banks's fabulous new series about three strong and sexy heroes. Book one is *Millionaire Dad*—and it's a story you won't want to miss. Next, meet the first of a few good men and women in uniform in the passion-filled new series BACHELOR BATTALION, by Maureen Child. The first installment, *The Littlest Marine,* will utterly delight you.

Continuing this month is the next book in Peggy Moreland's series TEXAS BRIDES about the captivating McCloud sisters, *A Sparkle in the Cowboy's Eyes.* And rounding out the month are two wonderful novels—*Miranda's Outlaw* by Katherine Garbera, and *The Texas Ranger and the Tempting Twin* by Pamela Ingrahm.

I hope you enjoy all six of Silhouette Desire's love stories this month—and every month.

Regards,

Melissa Senate

Melissa Senate
Senior Editor Silhouette Books

Please address questions and book requests to:
Silhouette Reader Service
U.S.: 3010 Walden Ave., P.O. Box 1325, Buffalo, NY 14269
Canadian: P.O. Box 609, Fort Erie, Ont. L2A 5X3

LEANNE BANKS
MILLIONAIRE DAD

SILHOUETTE *Desire*®
Published by Silhouette Books
America's Publisher of Contemporary Romance

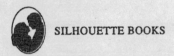

SILHOUETTE BOOKS

ISBN 0-373-76166-X

MILLIONAIRE DAD

This edition published by arrangement with Harlequin Books S.A.

® and TM are trademarks of Harlequin Books S.A., used under license. Trademarks indicated with ® are registered in the United States Patent and Trademark Office, the Canadian Trade Marks Office and in other countries.

Printed in U.S.A.

Books by Leanne Banks

Silhouette Desire

‡*Ridge: The Avenger* #987
**The Five-Minute Bride* #1058
**The Troublemaker Bride* #1070
**The You-Can't-Make-Me Bride* #1082
†*Millionaire Dad* #1166

‡ Sons and Lovers
* How To Catch a Princess
† The Rulebreakers

Silhouette Special Edition

A Date with Dr. Frankenstein #983
Expectant Father #1028

LEANNE BANKS

is a national number-one-bestselling author of romance.
She lives in her native Virginia with her husband and son
and daughter. Recognized for both her sensual and
humorous writing with two Career Achievement Awards
from *Romantic Times* magazine, Leanne likes creating a
story with a few grins, a generous kick of sensuality and
characters that hang around after the book is finished.
Leanne believes romance readers are the best readers in
the world because they understand that love is the greatest miracle of all. You can write to her at P.O. Box 1442,
Midlothian, VA 23113. An SASE for a reply would be
greatly appreciated.

This book is dedicated to the millionaire whose heart is as big as his bank account.

Prologue

"**H**ow come you're so good at math?"

"I dunno." Joey Caruthers shrugged as he finished showing the tricks of long division to nine-year-old Ben. "It makes sense."

Math made sense, but there were an awful lot of other things that didn't make sense to him. Like why his mom had to work two jobs, and they still never seemed to have enough money. Or why he didn't have a dad.

He glanced at the three other boys in the tree house. They lived on Cherry Lane in nice houses with moms and dads. They had puppies and kittens, and new clothes whether they wanted them or not. They had shiny new bikes and played Little League baseball. They wore the hottest tennis shoes. They visited interesting places like the shore or Disney World on family vacations.

Joey lived in a small apartment several blocks away. He had a goldfish once, but it died. His mom said his feet grew too fast, so his shoes were tight. He had to ride an old, rusted bike to get to Cherry Lane. His mom said he couldn't play Little League because she couldn't drive him to practice, and the uniforms were too expensive.

When he grew up, it would be different. He would have a dog and a big house and different tennis shoes for every day of the week. It all came down to math and money, and Joey was good at math. If he was good at math, then he figured he could be good at money.

For now, though, he didn't really belong to the "club." But he liked the tree house. Being in it was almost like taking a vacation to somewhere far away. The tree house could be anything the boys wanted it to be. He liked these guys. Being around them made him feel better on the inside. Sometimes he even forgot about the stuff that bothered him.

Joey figured if he kept showing up, maybe they would let him stay.

Ben looked at Stan. "Are you ready?"

Stan glanced at Nick, then at Joey and nodded. "It's time."

Joey got a weird feeling in the pit of his stomach. The guys were staring at him, and he wondered if they'd finally found out where he lived, or worse, that he didn't have a dad at all. He swallowed over a knot in his throat and stood.

"Time for what?" he asked when he couldn't stand it any longer.

Stan stepped in front of him and just stood there for a long moment.

Joey felt his stomach turn again, but he was careful not to show it. Stan was the oldest, and the tree house was in his yard. Joey was as big as Stan, but Stan was older by one year, and he was smart.

Stan motioned the two other boys closer.

"We're inviting you to become an official member of the Bad Boys Club. We'll teach you the secret handshake, and the password."

Shock and joy raced through Joey like an electric toy train. He was so excited he couldn't say a word.

"You gotta promise never to tell the secrets, and to stand up for a club member when he needs it."

Joey swallowed. "I promise," he managed solemnly.

"Your secret name is Joey 'Cash' Caruthers," Ben told him. "'Cause you're good in math."

Wow! he thought, but didn't say it because it wouldn't have been cool. Joey just nodded. "What are your names?"

"I'm Bad Ben," Ben said with an evil grin. "'Cause I get in trouble at school a lot."

"I'm Stan the Man, because I'm the oldest," Stan told him.

"And I'm Nail 'em Nick," the smallest guy said.

"Why Nail 'em?"

Nick shrugged. "I liked the way it sounded."

"And the handshake—"

"Stanley," a man's voice called from the ground. "It's time to go."

Stan's eyes rounded. "Freak! I forgot." He raced to the window. "I'll be right down, Dad," he yelled. "I think all the guys can go."

He turned back around to Joey. "My dad's taking us to the new space movie. You wanna go?"

The new space movie was supposed to be very cool. Everyone in school was talking about it.

"You oughta go," Ben said. "Maybe you could call your mom."

Joey's heart sank. His mom told him to only call her in case of emergency. She was afraid of getting fired. "I don't know," he said. "She has a real important job, and it's hard to get her sometimes."

Nick made a face. "Could you call your dad?"

Joey immediately shook his head and gave his usual answer. "He's traveling again."

"Well, maybe my dad would drive you by your house, and you could leave a note for your mom."

Panic raced through him. He didn't want the guys to know where and how he lived. "Nah, she'd get mad. I'd better go another time," he said, even though he knew another time would never come.

"You sure?" Stan asked. "My dad's treating all of us because I got all As on my report card."

Something in Stan's eyes made Joey think Stan knew more about him than he wanted him to know. An ugly feeling tightened his chest and settled in his stomach. It was the feeling he hated most in the world. Shame. Cramming his fists in his pockets, he shook his head. "Nah. I better not go this time."

Stan paused. "Okay. You wanna stay up in the tree house while we're gone? Now that you're a member, you can stay here by yourself."

Joey nodded. "Yeah, that sounds good. What's the password?"

Stan exchanged a look with the other boys and grinned. "We change it every week. This week, it's 'greasy, grimy gopher guts.'"

Joey nodded and grinned. "Okay. And the handshake?"

"Stanley, we need to leave for the movie!" Stan's dad called again.

"Okay, but we'll have to do it fast."

Ben and Stan folded their hands in an intricate series of movements, then each spit on the ground.

"Practice it while we're gone!" Nick said, and the boys hustled down the boards that served as a ladder.

"Don't let anybody in!" Ben called.

"Especially girls," Nick added.

"Okay," Joey said. "Tell me about the movie tomorrow."

"Okay!" they chorused.

He closed the trap door, and from the window he watched the boys run toward Stan's father's car. Within a couple of minutes they were gone.

The spring breeze blew over his face while he stared out the window. He loved it up here. He could be anything or anyone he wanted to be.

He spotted Stan's father's car turning out of the neighborhood and made a promise to himself. "When I grow up, it'll be different."

One

The stranded motorist was wrestling with a Honda Civic in a snowdrift on the side of the road.

The snowdrift was winning.

Inside his warm four-wheel-drive Suburban, Joe Caruthers slowed and watched the small person stomp out of the vehicle and kick a tire.

Looking more closely, he *guessed* it was a she. Hard to tell with the bulky coat, scarf and hat. She moved like a woman, though, and while Joe had great luck with money, he'd had god-awful misfortune with women. He drew them like honey drew bees, only they weren't after his honey; they'd always been after his cash.

Glancing at his cell phone, he figured he could call a towing company for her. Unfortunately, half of

Denver was stranded on the side of the road, so Miss Honda would have a long wait.

He thought of the conversation he'd just had with his longtime pal Sam Stewart and sighed. In his unique and wonderful way, Sam had told Joe again that if he didn't start getting involved with people, Joe would end up a lonely old, cold millionaire, and no one would come to his funeral except his golden retriever, Dixie.

Joe didn't give a rip who came to his funeral, but the lonely, cold part nagged at him. The tiny self-doubt he usually succeeded in burying bobbed to the surface like a fishing bob. Maybe he should give this good-neighbor nonsense a try. Swearing under his breath, he pulled his car to the side and got out. The cold air hit him in the face as he heard her talking to her Honda.

"This is crazy. It's not supposed to snow when it's three days away from May. And why aren't you skimming the surface of the snow the way the leasing agent told me you would?"

"Because your car has a low center of gravity," he told her. "The more you spin, the deeper she digs into the snow."

Her head whipped around, and her mouth dropped open. Wide blue eyes full of chagrin met his, and Joe felt an odd tingling inside him. It took him a minute before he realized it was the same sensation he experienced when he'd been dealt a winning hand of cards.

"'She'?" the woman finally repeated. "Is this

along the same lines as how they used to name hurricanes after women?''

"Something like that,'' Joe said. "Did you do any damage to your foot?''

Her cheeks turned deeper pink. "You weren't supposed to see that,'' she told him, her lips twitching. "Not one soul has passed here for the past hour. I'm not the type to kick tires.''

He chuckled at her exasperated tone. "Your secret's safe with me. Need a push?''

She sighed, and he felt a corresponding expansion inside himself. Even though she was tense, she looked real.

Accustomed to clever women with polished smiles and womanly wiles, Joe didn't see the quality very often, so he couldn't help staring. She looked like the kind of woman who wouldn't mind if the right man messed up her hair with his fingers.

Honest, he thought, then immediately dismissed that notion. Joe was convinced that honesty and women didn't go together. He had a theory that females lost the ability to tell the flat-out, honest truth around age thirteen.

Miss Honda did, however, look cautious. Not a bad thing, he thought, and approved her intelligence. He extended his hand. "Joe Caruthers. If you'd be more comfortable calling someone on my cell phone, you're welcome to it, but you'll probably have to wait for service.''

She winced and shook his hand. "Bad all over, huh?'' she murmured in a voice that was husky around the edges. "Thanks for stopping. I'm Marley."

He nodded, taking in her pink nose and cheeks. Blond curls, dusted with snow, escaped the confines of her knit hat. Even her eyelashes had a few white flakes on them. It took him a moment to figure out what was missing. "Makeup," he muttered under his breath. The woman wasn't wearing any makeup.

"Pardon?" she asked, glancing at him warily.

"Nothing," he said with a shrug. The directness of her gaze unsettled him, and he had the odd sense she could read his mind. He sure as hell didn't like that, so he turned his attention to her car. "New to Colorado," he guessed. "No snow tires. No cell phone."

"And rusty hazardous-driving skills," she finished for him. "I moved here a few weeks ago, but I haven't driven a car in years. The subway took me everywhere I needed to go."

Nodding, Joe grabbed a couple of mats from the back of his car and crouched down to place them under her tires. "If you're going to stay in Colorado, you should consider getting something with four-wheel-drive."

"I didn't think I would need it until next winter."

Rising, Joe shot her a look of pity. "We've had snow on the Fourth of July."

Dismay crossed her face. "July? Snow in July?"

"It's usually gone in a few hours. What made you pick Colorado?" he asked, because she clearly was no snow bunny.

She hesitated, and a hint of pain and disappointment deepened her eyes. The emotion was so honest and quick he felt it echo inside him. It caught him off guard.

"I needed to make a change," she said in a soft, wistful voice.

He nodded slowly. "I can understand that. It's happened once or twice to me." He felt the tingling again and frowned. Knocking on the hood of her Honda, he said, "If you'll get in, I'll give you a push and get you on your way."

"Yes, of course." She moved too quickly and slipped, a little sound of distress escaping her throat.

Joe automatically reached out, pulling her up and against him. Her remarkable blue eyes fixed on him. They stared at each other for several seconds. Out of nowhere a wicked, illicit thought snuck through his mind. He wondered if she would wear that same expression during sex. When a man slipped inside her, would she look at him as if he were the most important thing in her existence?

Despite the cold, her body felt warm. His skin felt hot. Despite the fact that *she* was the one who'd fallen, *he* felt off balance.

"Do you often do this?" she asked breathlessly.

"Do what?" he asked, inhaling deeply. Even her scent got under his skin.

"Rescue women."

Joe's brain kicked in. "Never," he said, coming to his senses and pulling away.

"Thank you for making an exception," she said, and hesitated. "I've got to tell you I'm not usually incompetent or helpless."

"I'm sure you're not," Joe told her as he opened her door. He wanted to get the hell away from her. All he'd intended to do was be a decent human being for a few minutes. If this was the result, he had no interest in repeating the experience. "You're fully liberated and self-sufficient," he said.

Sliding into the seat, she cocked her head to one side. "I don't know if I'd say self-sufficient. Hopefully self-actualized."

"Sounds like shrink rap to me," he muttered.

A pause, heavier than the wet, heavy snow, followed. "I am a psychologist."

Oh, hell. He'd stepped straight into that mess. "Well, it takes all kinds," he said. "Somebody's gotta listen to people's problems, just like somebody's gotta pick up the garbage. Might as well get paid for it."

She blinked, speechless for a full moment. "And what do you do?"

He closed her car door, but continued to watch her as she rolled down her window. Usually when he told women about his business, he could see the dollar signs flashing in their eyes. "I own some Rocky Mountain Steak Restaurant franchises."

She nodded slowly. "That's an important service, providing people with food and entertainment."

Her response wasn't what he'd expected, and the knowledge unsettled him again. "Yeah," he said with a shrug. "Most everyone likes steak."

"Most."

Hearing conditional agreement in her tone, he studied her. "And you?"

"I'm a vegetarian," she said with a smile that was different than her other one. This one was a little lopsided, yet sexy at the same time. "Steak is a fatty food which causes clogged arteries, heart attacks and ultimately death."

That stopped him. He shook his head and half chuckled. "I guess that would make me a murderer."

She gave a quick little shrug. "Nah. No more than an accessory."

The woman was clearly missing some of her Froot Loops. "You've got a different way of looking at things."

She nodded, and her smile broadened, pulling his gut tighter. "Hope so. I think everyone's a little insane. I just try to enjoy my insanity."

"Yeah, well—" he scratched his head "—have fun. Try putting the car in neutral, then ease into first."

"Thanks, Joe," she called after him in that husky voice he suspected would be ringing in his ears the rest of the night.

Joe got behind the Honda, and with all his might, he pushed the most disturbing woman he'd ever met right out of his life.

Marley's heart was pumping so hard she had to take several deep breaths. As she slipped and swerved over the snow-covered road, she wished she could say her physical reaction was due to the weather.

But it wasn't.

It was because that man had insulted her.

Marley heard an internal buzzer go off. *Wrong.* She was accustomed to cracks made about her profession. She'd made a few of her own.

She scowled. Okay, it was because, if she wasn't mistaken, that attractive, extremely sexual man had looked at her as if he wouldn't mind having her for breakfast. She shook her head. She knew she didn't inspire that kind of passion in a man, especially one that looked like him.

She could have dismissed the compelling combination of his dark, wavy hair, intense brown eyes, and smoothly chiseled bone structure. She could have gotten past the broad shoulders and muscular strength his jacket didn't hide. The hint of a Southern drawl in his voice that poured over her nerve endings like warm honey might have been a little tougher to forget.

The man's fatal charm, however, was that he had a sense of humor, not just about others, but about himself. *Killer* quality.

Gripping the steering wheel so tightly her hands began to cramp, Marley took a deep breath. It had been a long time since a man had looked at her that way, a long time since she'd let anyone past her defenses for even a moment.

It felt good, she told herself. She should accept it for what it was. A momentary lift to her flagging feminine spirits, and she'd certainly had reason to feel like a failure in that department lately. It was a common myth that psychologists had their act together in every way, Marley had learned. She had reached the conclusion that part of her purpose in life was to dispel that myth because she sure as heck didn't have her act together in every way. Especially with men over the age of twenty-five.

The Honda slid dangerously close to another drift. Driving demanded all her attention. ''No, no, no! Don't go there,'' she pleaded, wrenching the steering wheel in the opposite direction. ''Don't—''

Marley plowed into her second drift of the day. Swearing, she jerked the gear into reverse and spun her wheels. She tried rocking, shifting between reverse and neutral, but she only succeeded in imbedding the car deeper into the snow.

When she smelled burning rubber from the friction on her tires, she stopped and rested her forehead on the steering wheel. Lord, she was tired. To cap off the past six disastrous months of her life, four weeks ago, her nagging chest cold had turned out to be pneumonia. Her cough was gone, but her energy level was still zip. The sense of failure she'd desperately been fighting returned like an insidious fog.

''Oh, stop. As long as I don't freeze to death, it's going to get better,'' she muttered to herself.

She lifted her head, glanced in her rearview mirror and spotted a red Suburban pulling to a stop behind her. Her heart sank, then picked up. This was *not* her definition of better.

Within a moment he stood beside her car. She slowly rolled down her window.

He shook his head. ''I'll have to tow you this time.'' His rough-and-ready gaze met hers, a hint of a bad-boy grin lifting his lips. ''You think you can stand getting your car hauled by a man who causes heart attacks for a living?''

By the time Joe towed her car to the front of her small rental home, it was dark. Too dark. Marley noticed the lack of lights in the neighborhood and stifled a sigh. No power. She would much prefer to curl up and go to sleep in his warm car, but she pushed open her door and got out. ''What a day,'' she murmured, and locked her knees when she almost sank to the snow-covered ground.

''That your firewood beside the house?'' Joe asked as he unhooked her car from his.

Marley shivered beneath her coat and nodded.

''You'll need it.''

She dragged herself toward the woodpile, but Joe quickly strode past her and picked up some logs and kindling. ''I'll do it,'' he said, turning toward the house.

Marley watched him for a moment, then joined him on the porch. There was a reluctant, yet not quite grudging, sense of purpose to him. ''You've been very generous. You don't need to do any more.''

''I'll start the fire for you.''

''You really don't need—''

''You look like you're going to fall flat on your face. You'll freeze to death, and I'll be responsible. I see a battery-powered lantern's on top of the wood. You'll need it once you get inside.''

It was tough to muster indignation when her head felt like slush and her feet like lead. She shook her head and reached for the lantern. "Do you always go with the worst-case scenario?"

He met her gaze, and she saw a glimpse of many layers. Marley felt a quick buzz of awareness. Complex in a more-than-tough way, and unabashedly masculine with enough heat to burn a woman to cinders, this was not the boy next door. She'd always avoided this kind of man before.

"I've been through a few worst cases of my own."

Marley nodded.

His dark eyes grew wary. "No shrink stuff," he warned as if he knew she was wondering about him.

Marley lifted her hand in a dismissive gesture, then stepped forward to unlock the door. "No need to worry. I work with kids. The Jelly Bean Reward System doesn't work well with adults."

"Jelly beans?"

"Skittles, M&Ms, Sweet Tarts, Gummi Bears, Tootsie Rolls," she said as she led the way into her cold, dark house and flicked on the lantern.

"No Zotz?" he asked, moving directly to her fireplace.

Marley smiled. "You're showing your age. I miss Sugar Babies. I'm called the 'candy lady.'"

His gaze flicked over her with a subtle male curiosity. "'Candy lady,'" he repeated in a voice that gave a sensual edge to her nickname.

Marley felt her chest tighten and held her breath. "The kids," she finally managed. "The kids I treated called me that."

"Uh-huh," he said, and even that noncommittal

sound made her nerve endings stand on end. "I'm surprised a health food freak would use candy as a reward. Think of all the cavities."

Marley chuckled in relief at his gentle ribbing. "Cavities can be filled. Besides, I'm not a health food freak. I just don't eat much meat, especially beef."

Joe shook his head. "That's un-American."

"Now you sound like my father."

"Oh, really? What does he think of your career choice?"

"He thinks it's a little weird, but since I work with kids, he doesn't make too much noise. He wasn't happy about my moving to Colorado, though."

Joe shrugged and turned back to the fireplace. "As long as you're making more money—"

"Oh, I'm not. I took a cut. This move isn't about money."

He looked over his shoulder at her. "It's always about money."

Aha, Marley thought. One of those. "For a dyed-in-the-wool capitalist, it might always be about money. For me, it's not."

He narrowed his eyes and paused. "Bet you voted Democrat in the last election."

"Wrong again. I wrote in my dad's name. He's the last honest man in the country."

His eyebrows furrowed, and he gave a slight shake of his head. "Go ahead and sit down. You look wrecked."

She laughed to herself and sank onto the sofa. Except for the light from the lantern, the room was all shadows. She was still too cold to remove a stitch of her clothing. "Careful," she said. She had clearly been mistaken. He hadn't been looking at her *that* way. "All that flattery will go to my head."

"I'm sure you get your share of flattery," he said.

"Particularly from thirteen- and fourteen-year-old males. They like to try out their lines on someone safe."

He chuckled. "I remember those days. Are you always so trusting?"

"Because I got into your car?" she asked and watched him nod. "I follow my instincts and try to use my head. You were reluctant, but determined to help. Plus there's the fact that I'm not your type."

He stopped and turned to look at her, his dark eyebrows arched. "You're not?"

Marley's heart flipped at the "bad wolf" undertone in his voice, then she took a breath. She'd almost been fooled again. "That's right," she managed. "If we were at a party with twenty other people, ten women and ten men, I would be the last woman you would hit on."

"And why is that?" he asked in a mild voice.

Marley refused to get nervous. "Because you're a man who clearly appreciates the finer things. You drive a very nice car, dress in designer clothing, probably live in a luxurious house. I would guess you're accustomed to finely wrapped women who appreciate your material accomplishments."

He looked slightly disconcerted, but he didn't deny a word she'd said. "Are you saying you're not a finely wrapped woman or that you don't appreciate material accomplishments?''

Marley smiled. "I know I'm not finely wrapped. Just average. Don't get me wrong. Wrapping can be nice. It just doesn't hold my interest very long. I think material accomplishments can be a sort of wrapping. I've always been much more interested in what's inside the package instead of outside.'' She stifled a yawn and chuckled. "Aren't you glad you asked?''

He cocked his head to one side and looked at her with an assessing expression on his face. "I'll have to think about that,'' he told her, then turned back to the fireplace.

Marley sighed and relaxed into the couch. Struggling with heavy eyelids, she quietly watched him set and light the fire. She knew it was just wrapping, but his rear end was pretty darn good. The leather jacket suited him, as did the well-fitting jeans. She must be dizzy, she thought, because she was seriously considering telling him he had a great rear end even if his disposition needed some work.

She covered a yawn, and when her eyes drifted closed, a fantasy danced through her mind of him holding her in his arms. It had been a while since someone had held her, and the image warmed her all the way through.

Yawning again, she shifted slightly and put her arms around herself. "It's tough being a hero, isn't it?''

Hero. Joe immediately rejected the notion, but paused before he said anything. "I'm a lot of things, but I sure as hell am no hero," he muttered, and turned around to set her straight. "You were right about some of—"

He broke off when he saw that she had fallen asleep. With the firelight playing over her features, he looked at her for a long moment. The color had gone out of her cheeks, making her appear delicate and younger. She gave the impression of feminine strength when she talked, but now, looking as if she was giving herself a hug, she looked incredibly vulnerable.

Joe wondered at the source of her strength and the cause of her vulnerability. He wondered why he was curious and decided it must be timing. Sam Stewart's tongue-lashing about his not getting involved with anyone was making him do a lot of useless self-evaluating. It would pass.

For now, though, he would finish his good deed. Joe wondered if he could get the candy lady out of her wet clothes without waking her. A challenge. He'd always enjoyed a challenge.

Kneeling closer, he started with her wet shoes and socks. He shook his head at the thin dark socks. He slid his hand up her calves and carefully rolled down her socks to reveal her small, pretty feet. When she arched her foot in his hand, he glanced up at her face, but her eyes were still closed.

He removed the silly knit gloves finger by finger. The woman clearly needed a lesson on how to dress for the elements. Her cool hands were well groomed, but bare of fingernail polish. No surprise there. He would bet she didn't dye her hair, either.

Her wool pea coat was trickier. He had to disengage her from the hug position, unfasten her buttons, then tug the sleeves free. He was surprised at her body. He'd expected slim lines, but she had curves.

His mouth twisted slightly. Her clothes, however, did nothing to accentuate her shape. Interesting, he thought. Her breasts weren't full, but another expression came to mind. One she wouldn't approve of, he thought. More than a handful. Her hips curved from her waist in a way that made him wonder what it would be like to know her more intimately.

He shook his head. He wouldn't, of course. He was just determined to finish his good deed of the decade. Spotting the quilt on the back of the sofa, he carefully tucked it around her. He pulled her wool cap from her head, and her blond waves spilled free to her shoulders.

His fingers buzzed with the winning sensation again. If Joe believed in magic, he would say there was magic in her little house tonight. Joe had given up on magic a long time ago, but there was something different in the air. Something more than a freak spring snowstorm.

Marley was an unusual woman, and he was intrigued. Was it possible that a woman could look at him and see him instead of his money? Giving in to the urge to touch a silky lock, Joe stared at her for a long moment. He hadn't seen a more-innocent-looking woman in years. But he'd learned the hard way that appearances could be deceiving.

Two

"If I took this personally, my ego would be six feet under. I don't make a habit of putting women to sleep, at least, not at the beginning of the evening."

Still struggling with heavy lids, and vaguely disoriented, Marley blinked. She heard the sexy masculine humor in Joe's low, rough voice. Her gaze locked with his, and a surge of adrenaline curled through her.

"I'm sorry. It's nothing personal," she said, sitting up and pulling the quilt with her. Pushing her hair from her face self-consciously, she shook her head at herself. "I had a touch of pneumonia a month ago, and I haven't quite gotten my energy level back."

The firelight played over him, accenting his height and broad shoulders. He stood looking down at her with his hands resting loosely on his hips. "The altitude might be getting to you, too. It affected me when I first moved here."

The altitude? Marley liked that explanation better than some of the other possibilities skipping through her mind. She noticed her socks and shoes lined up in front of the fire along with her coat. An image of Joe touching her bare feet made her toes curl. She looked at his square fingers and strong hands. Too aware of how he loomed over her, she moved to rise, but he immediately put a hand on her shoulder.

"No need to get up," he assured her with a gentle expression in his eyes that sent her in another circle.

The man confused the stuffing out of her. One moment he was all hard edges, the next he was so kind he took her breath away. "You've been too kind, done too much. I thought you said you didn't make a habit of helping."

He shrugged, then scowled. "I don't. You're my one good deed of the decade. I had just finished getting a lecture from one of my friends about how I need to get more involved with people, just before I drove past you."

Marley laughed. She'd missed the boat again. His attention was purely impersonal, purely an act of charity. "Well, I'm not sure how I won the lottery on this one, but thank you again. I think." She stood. "Would you like some hot chocolate?"

He hesitated.

"With my electricity out, I can't offer much in the way of a meal. If you have somewhere else to be, I'll understand."

He shook his head. "Just some paperwork at home, and my power's probably out, too."

"Your reluctance is incredibly flattering," she told him. "Here's the offer. Cocoa and conversation. After that, I won't call you. You won't call me. We'll never see each other again."

His gaze was a mixture of speculation and approval. "Okay."

Grabbing the lantern, Marley nodded and headed for the kitchen. He must not receive that kind of offer often, she thought wryly. "You spend so much time working, you don't have much left over for relationships. Right?" she said over her shoulder.

"Yeah," he muttered as he followed her.

Her lips twitched in irony at his wary tone. "Don't worry," she told him, collecting the chocolate mix, mugs, and filling a kettle with water. "I'm not working up a chart on you. That's empathy you hear in my voice. I've had the same problem of getting lost in my work, and I've received some similar—" she paused, searching for a kinder, gentler word than *nagging* or *criticism* "—suggestions."

"You have a friend who nags the hell out of you, too?"

"My father. He tells me if I don't cut out some of my work and spend some time with men of marriageable age instead of preadolescents, I'll end up a lonely, old maid. Then I tell him I'd rather end up by myself than permanently attached to someone I don't like, let alone love." Marley smiled grimly. "My mother usually tries to step in before we draw blood."

She felt a stab of sadness, and worse, the residual sting of failure. "I thought I had it all taken care of when I got engaged six months ago, but—" She broke off, wondering what in heaven's name had possessed her to rattle on and on. "Sorry," she said, returning to the den. "I'll be putting you to sleep soon. What about you? Does your family live in Denver?"

He shook his head, his gaze again showing a depth that sent an answering ripple inside her. "No family now. I was raised in Virginia."

No family now. Marley thought that would explain his strongly independent presence. A loner, she thought, and decided to tread carefully on the subject of his family.

She hung the kettle over the fire, then grabbed her candy dish and sat in front of the fire. "Have a seat. I thought I heard a trace of a Southern accent."

Joe joined her on the floor. "I've lived all over since I grew up. What happened to your engagement?"

Marley stiffened, then automatically took a breath to relax. Playing with the wrapped candy, she told herself she didn't need to impress Joe. After tonight she wouldn't see him again. The knowledge was freeing. "It didn't work out. He thought I was too committed to my work, and—"

"And?" Joe prompted, his brown eyes demanding truth.

She looked at him again. He emanated intensity in the way he talked, the way he moved, the way he looked at her. He had a strong sense of power and wouldn't hesitate to use it. If he wanted a woman, she would know just by the way he looked at her. Her stomach took a dip, and she quickly reminded herself that Joe wouldn't want her that way.

She glanced away from him to the candy. "And he was probably right." She couldn't hold back a wince. "The truth is my work was more interesting and rewarding to me. Don't get me wrong. He was a nice man, well grounded in his career, always on an even keel…"

"And he bored the hell out of you."

"I didn't say that," she said.

"But you thought it."

"I feel like I'm speaking ill of the dead," she said, biting back laughter and shaking her head.

"I bet he didn't do a thing for you in bed, either."

Feeling her cheeks heat from the accuracy of his remark, Marley closed her eyes. "I take the fifth on that one."

"No passion," he said.

"Passion fades," Marley returned, opening her eyes to meet his gaze.

His mouth lifted slightly in something sexier than a grin, and he leaned closer. "But it's not boring."

For a sliver of a second she was trapped by her fascination with him. His eyes held her as easily as his arms would have. It was a strange and new sensation for Marley.

She had the deep sense that Joe's ego and mind were fiercely strong. She wouldn't have to coddle him. He would meet her toe-to-toe. A flutter of excitement ran though her, and suddenly she was daring herself again. It was the best feeling in the world for Marley, and it had been missing for too long.

She tossed a piece of candy at him.

He caught it easily and cocked his head to one side, his gaze curious. She wondered how he seemed to burn with masculine energy.

"Tootsie Roll for your story?" she said.

"Is this how the candy lady gets her way?"

She couldn't hold back a smile. "I gave Tootsie Rolls, inexpensive trinkets and video-game time in exchange for specific, accomplished tasks. Cooperation was rewarded."

"And did you reward your fiancé with Tootsie Rolls?"

Marley felt a sting inside her again. Her smile faded, but she met his gaze. "No. I rewarded him with my undivided attention."

"He must have been highly motivated."

"Cooperation wasn't his forte."

Joe nodded. "Oh. A bore *and* a pain in the butt."

"Your words," she said, lifting her hand.

"Your thoughts," he returned.

"Your turn," she said, then reached for the hot water to mix the hot chocolate. The fire crackled, but Joe was silent. "Okay. Fill in the blanks. Once upon a time a baby boy named Joe was born in—"

"Roanoke, Virginia. Is this what you do with your clients?"

"Don't be stingy. I told you my story. Roanoke, Virginia, where he lived until—"

"—he graduated from high school and completed one year of college. He ran out of money and—"

Joe paused, clearly choosing his words "—decided to seek his fortune."

"His mother and father were sad to see Joe leave, but—"

"His mother was sad to see Joe leave," Joe corrected. "But she had worked two and three jobs for a long time to support them, so Joe didn't want to be a burden anymore."

"And Joe's father?" Marley watched his eyes darken and sensed the pain immediately.

He hesitated a long moment and looked away. "Never knew him."

Oh, that hurt. If she'd been in a session, she would have explored that more. Tonight, however, wasn't about therapy, and she wasn't interested in rubbing a raw place. She took a breath and went on. "When Joe was a little boy, he was very good at—"

His lips quirked. "Math."

Marley winced and handed him his mug. "I could hate you for that. I had to take algebra twice."

He lifted an eyebrow. "I'm sure you had other talents."

Marley held her breath. He was probably one of those men who had at least one sexual thought every thirty seconds, because he oozed sexuality. Although she was accustomed to diffusing sexual tension with her clients, right now she had to concentrate to keep from stuttering. "When Joe left home to seek his fortune, he went to—"

"Las Vegas," he told her, and she could feel him watching her carefully. "He made his first fortune playing blackjack."

Marley stared at him in surprise. "You're joking!"

He chuckled. "No. I was always good at math, and blackjack is a game of math."

"You must have been very good."

"Good enough to get thrown out of a few casinos."

"A gambler," she murmured, still fascinated and not totally surprised.

"A specialist in risk evaluation."

She laughed. "Is that what you put on your tax return?"

He shrugged and took a sip of the chocolate. "Something like that."

"Blackjack," she said, and thought of the cards in the end table drawer. "Would you teach me?"

"You don't know how to play?"

"Not blackjack." She waved her hand dismissively. "I've been too busy getting my Ph.D. and learning Nintendo. I don't know many adult games."

"You don't know many adult games. I could interpret that several ways."

"I'm sure you could, but how about if we stick to blackjack?" She scooted over to an end table and pulled out a deck. "Here you go," she said, setting the deck in front of him. "I don't ask for much. I just want to know all your secrets."

Joe just looked at her for a long moment, taking in the careless mane of her blond hair that shone in the firelight, along with the intelligence and warmth that sparkled in her eyes. Marley was a trip to the circus. She delighted him and almost scared him. Almost.

"I've already told you something I've never told anyone else," Joe said.

Her eyes widened in surprise. "Oh, really?"

"About my father."

She nodded. "And how does that feel?"

"I haven't decided," he muttered, taking another drink from his cocoa.

She gently smiled. "It gets easier after the first time," she said in a voice that rubbed over his skin like a cat purring.

Joe felt the buzz and hum running through him again. She was fully dressed, and so was he, yet he felt a strange intimacy. Maybe it was the firelight. Maybe it was just the night. Without intending to, she was weaving some kind of hot, sweet foreplay that started in his brain and spread.

He slid a glance to her bare feet and remembered how soft her skin was. He suspected she kept her sexuality under wraps. She was a cotton kind of lady, yet underneath it all she felt like silk. It was almost as if she wore a disguise but he knew her secret.

He reached out to touch a strand of her hair. "How do you usually wear your hair?"

Her blue gaze locked with his. "I pull it back in a clip or a braid. Why?"

His lips chipped upward. "That's what I expected. You hide your light under a bushel."

She shrugged her slim shoulders and dipped her head. "I have to get rid of distractions."

It was a novel concept for Joe that a woman would

play down her beauty so it wouldn't get in the way. She reminded him of an abstract picture that became clearer the longer he looked at it.

She lifted her eyebrows. "So, are you going to show me the tricks to blackjack or not?"

He'd like to show her a helluva lot more than blackjack. But he wouldn't. Conversation and cocoa was the deal. He drew back. "Okay. What are we playing for?"

Marley smiled, and he wondered why her expression seemed to slide down his gut. She might as well have scraped her fingernail down the zipper of his jeans.

She took a piece of candy from the dish, unwrapped it, and waved it at him. "Tootsie Rolls."

An hour of tutoring passed, and Joe was ready to wave the white flag. "I can't play one more game," he said, grabbing his stomach.

"Afraid you'll lose your Tootsie Rolls?" Marley said with a dirty chuckle.

"I thought the winner got to take the jackpot home." He leaned back and watched her.

Marley shook her head. "Oh no. You win, you eat. It's the least you could do since you smeared me. House rules."

He arched an eyebrow. "House rules?"

She lifted her chin a fraction of an inch. "My house. I rule."

He liked the way she didn't give an inch yet she was playful about it. She was a curious, challenging woman, and Joe reveled in a challenge. "If you want to try out your new—" he paused "—skills, there are some casinos within—"

The hall light flickered on, and the heating system thumped as it started. Marley's eyes widened. "Hallelujah! The power's on. This means I can use my electric blanket tonight, after all."

In Joe's opinion it was a damn shame Marley needed an electric blanket to keep her warm at night. He glanced at the empty mugs, then around the room, taking in the cozy comfort of her home. The sofa and chairs were sturdy, but well padded with cushions. The muted colors were accented with splashes of green and melon, making the room feel safe, yet stimulating.

He looked at Marley again and suspected the decor reflected her. A man could feel safe with her. His protectiveness immediately rose in protest. When had he ever felt truly safe? Safety was an illusion.

Impatient, he stood. He felt tugged in different directions. The night had been almost magic, but the light intruded.

Marley collected the mugs and followed him to her feet. "Time to go, or would you like one more mug of hot chocolate?"

He shook his head. "Thanks, but I should go."

She nodded and smiled. "Okay. Thank you for rescuing me. If you need proof of your good deed of the decade, you know where I am."

He felt as if he were leaving something unfinished, but had no clue what it was. He zipped his jacket and glanced down at her bare toes curling into the carpet. He shook his head. "Crazy night."

"Interesting," she murmured in agreement when he lifted his gaze to hers.

In her blue eyes he saw curiosity and a little of the strange wonder he was feeling. His gut tightened. If she were different, if he were different, he would want to see her again. He would want to know her in all the ways a man could know a woman.

He reached out to touch a strand of her hair, and she went very still. The air was heavy with what might have been—if they'd been different people. Joe looked at her mouth.

"You're not going to kiss me, are you?" she whispered.

Of course not, his rational side agreed. But he moved closer and lowered his head. "Don't worry," he told her, soothing both her and himself at the same time. "It's just a goodbye kiss."

She let out a long breath of relief. "Oh."

Sliding his fingers to the back of her head, he tilted her mouth upward and pressed his lips to hers. She tasted sweet from the cocoa, soft and warm. He slipped his tongue past her lips, and she responded by opening to him in a way that made his blood race.

He deepened the kiss still more, and a raging fire was threatening to burn between them. Mentally swearing, Joe pulled back and knew the arousal on her face was mirrored on his. He shook his head. This was crazy. It bothered the hell out of him to say the words, but he was determined.

"Goodbye, Marley. Take care." Then he walked out of her house.

* * *

Moments after he'd left, Marley was staring at the door. She felt as if she'd stood too close to the fire and gotten singed. Another moment passed before she realized she was still touching her lips.

Laughing, she jerked her hand away and swiped her hand across her forehead. "Crazy," she whispered to herself, amazed that her body was still in a riot.

She hadn't felt this way in such a long time. Or, she wondered, had she *ever* felt this way? She couldn't remember this edgy excitement for her ex-fiancé. Although she'd been reluctant to admit it, she'd wondered if the lack of chemistry between them had been part of their problem.

Frowning, Marley wrapped her arms around herself and walked to the fireplace to put out the fire for the night. Marley didn't believe in love at first sight. Love was like a flower. It started with a seed, and it needed water, sun and attention in order for it to grow. As a psychologist, she understood the stages of relationship development. Chemistry sizzled, then died.

Marley thought of Joe and how his dynamic personality had taken up her den. She could still feel his presence and the strange intimacy they'd shared.

An emotional one-night stand. Emotional sex, she thought.

"No," she said to herself, and adjusted the damper, then went to the bathroom. She washed her face, brushed her teeth and made a face at her wild hair before she went to her bedroom.

Inside the comfortable room she'd furnished to her

taste and for her pleasure, Marley stripped and put on a comfortable, but nonsexy, flannel nightgown. Since her feet were cold, she pulled on kneesocks, then slid beneath the thick, rose-colored down comforter and crisp cotton sheets.

Weariness sank into her bones and blood, and it wasn't long before she began to drift. Safe in the cocoon of sleep, she could see, be and do anything she wanted. The camera in her mind began to roll, and she found herself sitting on a cliff in the dark, waiting.

A man came to her. She couldn't see his face, but she could feel his intensity surround her like an ocean. He was ethereal, close enough to touch, but more vapor than substance. He wasn't real, she thought, but she could feel him on her skin and in her heart. It was strange to her that she could read him so well without seeing his face. It was almost as if he emitted a signal and she had the capacity to receive it.

He was dark and light and everything in between. In another circumstance she might have been afraid of him, but she sensed his wonder and even a little of his fear. What lured her most, however, was his passion. For her.

Not many people knew that Marley longed to want and be wanted in a way that surpassed everything she'd experienced in her life, even in her dreams. Not everyone knew that Marley wanted a man who possessed a passion that would push the limits.

Marley just knew she'd never found a man to match her. Had he finally found her?

Strong and dark, he twined his fingers through her hair and pulled her closer to him. No longer vapor, he was real. She could feel his heart pound, his breath on her face.

He urged her mouth to his, and she got lost in his taste. He held her tightly, letting her know he wouldn't easily release her. He pulled her intimately against him so she could feel he was hard with wanting her.

The power of his arousal made her dizzy. She had never been wanted like this before. Never. Staring into his dark eyes, Marley tried to breathe. Frustrated, she still couldn't see his face. She wanted to see him. More than anything, she *had* to know him.

"I want you," he said in a voice rough with desire.

Something inside her protested. She didn't believe in one-night stands. A one-night stand was like nitroglycerin—unstable, unpredictable emotionally and physically.

"I need you," he said and slid her dress from her shoulders. It pooled at her feet.

He touched her intimately, with sure but sweet strokes. His words made her crazy. She felt herself sinking, wanting more.

"I've got to have you," he told her, his need obliterating her objections. She wanted to possess and be possessed.

She clung to his shoulders and stared into his face, finally seeing him.

It was Joe, and he was inside her.

Three

"**T**his group of boys is going to put me into an early grave." Sam stabbed his fork into a medium-rare T-bone steak, compliments of one of Joe's restaurants.

Sitting across from Sam as he ate the take-out meal, Joe took his friend's complaint in stride. "You always say they start out like hellions, then improve by the end of the summer."

Sam shook his head and raked his hand through his thinning hair. "This group's different. They fight like cats and dogs. We've already had too many trips to the clinic, and I sure as hell don't want them killing each other on my turf."

Since the summer camp's inception, Sam operated the boys camp and Joe funded it. The two men had met during their gambling days. Joe had identified

Sam as an emotional gambler, which meant Sam hadn't been very successful. Sam was a gambler with heart, misplaced in the world of high stakes and high dollars. He was, however, terrific with kids.

Throughout the past three years, Sam had employed various methods for getting Joe more personally involved. Joe maintained that his money would be more helpful to the boys than his cynical attitude. He was no hero. The camp was a salve to the burning emptiness that he pushed past on a regular basis. He frowned.

"You need some help?" Joe asked. This time Sam appeared genuinely concerned.

"Yeah, I do," Sam said. "I heard some hotshot youth specialist from back East is at the university. I've called her twice, but she keeps saying she's not doing private practice anymore."

Joe felt a kick of electricity zip through him. He sat straighter in his chair. "Her name wouldn't be Marley—"

"Fuller," Sam said, pausing mid-bite. "Dr. Marley Fuller." He narrowed his eyes in doubt. "You've heard of her?"

"I met her." He'd met her, kissed her and fully intended to forget her. After all, they had only shared cocoa, conversation and a goodbye kiss. It wasn't as if they'd made love, he'd told himself over and over again. He had, however, been unable to dodge the gnawing sense in his gut that he'd never been so intimate with a woman.

Sam put his fork down. "You think you could talk

her into doing an assessment on these hellions? I'm at the end of my rope."

"What makes you sure she'll be able to help?" Joe asked, hanging on to his skepticism.

"You know those youth conferences you're always shipping me off to so I'll get the latest and the greatest information? Well, the speakers always quote Marley Fuller in their workshops. But she's always been too busy working to speak. She's supposed to be good. Damn good. She doesn't dish out a bunch of psychobabble. She's practical."

"Sounds like she walks on water," Joe said

"I don't care if she walks on marshmallows. Can you get her?"

Joe hesitated a long moment, objections firing from his mind like rounds from his hunting rifle. He and Marley weren't right for each other. They both knew that. So why had she crossed his mind every damn day since he'd met her? They'd made a deal that neither would call.

But some deals were made to be broken. She was beginning to feel like a bad case of poison ivy to him. The reason the woman was so distracting, Joe decided, was because the weather had been weird that night, and they'd spent the evening in the soft glow of firelight. In the clear light of day she wouldn't hold his attention.

He needed to get rid of the poison ivy. He nodded. "I can get her."

Sam arched his bushy eyebrows. "You know a lot of women, but this one doesn't fit your usual profile.

What makes you sure you can get her?''

Joe didn't pause. "She owes me."

"Behavior modification is an effective method for children to gain control of their anger,'' Marley said, addressing her last graduate-level course for the day. Over the past few weeks she'd learned she much preferred smaller groups. "Teaching self-awareness about initial physical responses to anger and appropriate coping skills is helpful, but providing an effective motivation is—''

Marley watched Joe Caruthers stroll into the classroom as if he owned it, and her mind went completely blank. Dressed in jeans that emphasized his lean height and a leather jacket that made her think of all the men she'd avoided, he took a seat and gave her a slow look full of challenge. He might as well have said, "Show me what you've got, sweetheart."

There was something about him that was blatantly sexual. She knew a sex-therapist colleague who would have a field day with his body language. Then again, her sex therapist friend had once told Marley she could win a prize for diffusing sexual advances.

Her heart banged against her rib cage as if she'd just mainlined ten cups of black coffee. A student's cough dragged her attention back to her class, half of whom were craning to see the man in the back. She overheard one of the younger female students remark to another, "Hunk alert."

Feeling her cheeks burn, she fought the urge to fiddle with her hair and tug at the collar of her dress. She longed for her jeans, sweatshirt and a roomful of juvenile delinquents. She would have felt infinitely more comfortable.

Taking a deep breath, she stared at her notes. "Providing an effective motivation is tricky," she finally managed. Tricky. So was Joe Caruthers. Wondering why he was here, she forced her attention back to the lecture and ruthlessly kept her gaze away from him.

Despite her best efforts, she stuttered and fumbled more during that lecture than any she'd given and gave a huge sigh of relief when she finished. A couple of students came forward to ask questions. When the last one left, Marley collected her notes and stopped trying to ignore Joe.

As she walked toward him, he stood. "How's it going, Dr. Candy? You like these older kids?"

"There are days that I miss my street gangs." She felt him inspect her thoroughly from head to toe and decided not to beat around the bush. "What brings you here?"

"I need your services," he told her in a way she suspected would bring many women to their knees.

Marley stiffened hers. "You need someone to teach a class on child psychology?"

"I need a hotshot expert from back East to come and evaluate why the current crop of campers at my summer camp isn't happy. I need this expert to give my camp director, Sam, a few suggestions. And I'll pay."

Marley blinked. "You have a summer camp?"

"For boys at risk. I set it up a few years ago." He lifted his hand. "Before you start thinking I'm a nice philanthropist type, all I do is fund it and take the tax deduction. My friend Sam Stewart does the real work.''

Marley's head was spinning, but she put a footnote on the way Joe diminished his generosity. ''That name Sam Stewart is familiar.''

He grinned. ''Yeah, you blew him off when you told him you weren't practicing anymore.''

Marley winced. ''I'm not. I've tried to make a clean break, but I keep getting calls, so I wrote this standard response that I keep next to my phone and read every time I get a request. I give referrals.''

''Sam's picky about the boys. He wants the best.''

She shot him a doubtful look and walked toward the door. ''Tall order.''

''From what I hear,'' he said in a deep voice as he walked beside her, ''it shouldn't be a problem for you.''

She could hear the sincerity in his tone. He wasn't flattering her. Marley felt a shimmering sensation inside her. ''What's the problem?''

''They're fighting,'' Joe said with a frown. ''Apparently more than usual. Since this is your last class today, let me take you to dinner, and I'll tell you about it.''

''I haven't agreed to anything,'' she warned him.

He chuckled. ''You will.''

Marley turned and met his gaze. ''What makes you so sure?''

He shrugged. ''Name your price,'' he said in the same voice that made her think of a hot night, tangling bodies and two hearts that pounded together, but his words rubbed her the wrong way.

"*If* I agree to do this, and I'm not saying I will, there won't be any money exchanged."

"We'll see."

"Yes, we will," she said, and glanced at her watch. "I need to pick up some papers from my office. Where should I meet you?"

"I'm not in a hurry. I can go with you."

Marley bit back her frustration. She wanted some distance, just a few moments to collect herself. A few moments when she didn't smell his aftershave or get distracted by his eyes. "Okay," she murmured, and they walked the short distance to her office.

Lynn, the young graduate teaching assistant assigned to Marley, gaped at Joe as they entered the small room. "Are you a student?" she asked, the expression on her gamine face flashing "Pay dirt."

Joe's mouth quirked to one side. "Not yet."

Marley tried to think of a polite way to tell Lynn her mouth was hanging open enough to catch flies. She wished the G.T.A. wouldn't be so obvious in her admiration of Joe. The man's ego was probably huge. "Lynn, this is Joe Caruthers. He's interested in a consultation."

"I thought you weren't doing any more," she said, her gaze never straying from Joe.

"I wasn't," Marley said glumly.

"She couldn't resist this one," Joe teased.

Lynn looked at Marley with new eyes. "I can see why she would make an exception."

Lord, she wasn't even going to try to follow up that. "Any messages?"

"Yes, two more people from out of state asking for consultations and your sister, Tina."

Marley did a double take and smiled. "Tina?"

"Yes," Lynn said, and jabbed a pencil behind her ear. "She said you need to start wearing heels. They will give you a more authoritative image."

Marley laughed and shook her head. "Now that I'm working with adults instead of children, my sister has become my self-appointed fashion consultant."

"You don't believe her?" Joe asked, glancing down her legs to her flats.

Self-conscious, Marley tucked a strand of hair into her loose French braid. "It's not that. I've had a lot of changes over the past several months, so I prefer to make other changes more gradually."

Joe smoothed his hand over the unruly strand. "And what does your sister say about your hair?"

"'Cut it off,'" Marley said cheerfully, despite the weird feeling in her stomach. She breathed again when he removed his hand.

She even managed to laugh at his scowl, then turned to Lynn. "Have a good weekend."

Lynn glanced at Joe and sighed. "Not as good as yours."

Marley opened her mouth to correct her assistant's absurd assumption, then decided time would take care of that for her. "Ready," she said to Joe, and they left.

Sweet Peter, she was so cute, Joe thought as he watched Marley grow increasingly flustered by the attention from the waiter at his restaurant. He'd always overlooked cute women for drop-dead beautiful. Shortsighted perhaps? Maybe, he thought with a sinking feeling in his gut, it was just *her*. Maybe Marley had some special quality he'd never found in other women. A disturbing thought, he pushed it aside and continued to watch her.

The waiter was trying to sell her on a cut of beef as if his life depended on it.

"They sound delicious," she said. "I'm sure your steaks are superior, but—"

"But?" The waiter's face fell.

Marley shot Joe a look of distress, then sighed. "I'm a vegetarian," she gently told him. "A salad and baked potato would be wonderful."

The waiter looked at her in confusion. "Oh," he said, finally recovering to ask her choice of salad dressing.

"I'll have the special," Joe said.

The waiter nodded in approval. "Prime rib. Rare."

When the waiter left, she shook her head and smiled. "You should have warned me we were going to one of your restaurants. How does it feel being king of the hill every time you walk into one of these?"

"I don't think about it much. I'm usually too busy looking for ways to improve." He touched a wilting plant on the table and waved the hostess over to replace it.

"Needs more sun," Marley told him.

"Needs something," he said, and the disturbing

thought struck him, as it often had lately, that he needed something, too. He turned his gaze back to her. "I like the dress."

She paused as if she were unaccustomed to compliments. "Thank you," she finally said.

"You should wear your hair down," he told her.

Her mouth curved in a tilted smile. "You're an image consultant, too?"

"No, just an admirer. It's a waste of natural resources for you to pull your hair back."

"I can't get used to seeing me without it pulled back. I guess I'm just going to have to oversleep one morning so I don't have time to fool with it."

"If you need a late night," Joe began, unable to resist pulling her chain a little.

"I'll watch a midnight monster movie," she said quickly, but her cheeks turned pink. "When can I observe your summer campers?"

"As soon as possible. Sam's ready to yell uncle."

"Tomorrow, then. It would also be helpful if you would share individual background information on the boys."

"Whatever you need."

She glanced at him doubtfully. "You're being very agreeable."

"I'm harmless."

"Uh-huh," she said in disbelief. "About as harmless as my sister, Tina, is. She's a Wall Street whiz who eats small companies for breakfast." She stopped abruptly. "Now Tina would interest you. Sharp, quick and a capitalist to the bone."

Joe shook his head. "I've got enough edges. Sam

tells me I should take a trip to the Wizard of Oz and get myself a heart.''

She tilted her head to one side considering him. ''That can't be completely true. I bet you initiated the idea for this summer camp.''

''Yeah,'' he reluctantly admitted. ''But it's a tax write-off.''

''You could have chosen other, easier ways for a tax write-off.''

Her persistence irritated him at the same time he admired it. ''Don't get the wrong idea. I'm no hero.''

She laughed and probably had no idea she made such a husky, sexy sound. ''You say *hero* like it's a terrible four-letter word. Face it. You're doing something terrific for those boys. That means that deep down in your capitalistic heart, you have some redeeming quality.''

''You've been a psychologist too long. Your brains have started to shrink.''

She made a tsking sound. ''Do you always lash out when someone tells you the truth about yourself? Don't worry. Your secret's safe with me,'' she said, lowering her voice to a whisper that affected him like an intimate touch. ''Joe Caruthers is a hero.''

The next day he watched her watch the boys. She'd dressed simply in a white T-shirt and jeans, and again pulled back her hair. She may have been trying to keep her appearance unobtrusive, but in the sunlight, her pale blond hair reminded him of a sparkler. Her facial expressions gave little hints to her mental concentration and emotions. The predominant one he read was compassion, and it tugged hard at something deep inside him.

A man would need to look two or three times to see her appeal. Joe saw it and kept looking.

During lunch she interviewed Sam and assured him that he was doing a good job. Sam was beaming by the time he finished his apple cobbler. That afternoon, when she played an interactive game with the boys and a few resisted, she pulled out the big guns. Plastic tarantulas for all who participated.

It was corny as hell, but she reminded him of a sunbeam. If he were in the mood to bet, he'd say every male she'd looked at with those baby blues of hers had a crush on her.

Except him.

Joe didn't have a crush on her. He just wanted to get inside those baby blues and find out why she made his hand tingle like he was holding a winning hand of cards. He wanted to get under her skin and find out if he shook her up—just a little. He wanted to take her to bed.

After he drove Marley to her little house, he walked her to her door, remembering the crazy, snowy night they'd shared. He had the same feeling tonight as he had then. He wanted more time with her. Not much, just a little more time with her.

He noticed she was lifting her shoulders as if they were tight. "Did you get some sore muscles today?"

She shrugged again and nodded. "Sometimes when I concentrate on something for an extended time, I get tense, and it shows up later. A shower and good night's rest should help."

"I've got a Jacuzzi at my house," he said.

"That's nice," she said with a smile.

He leaned against her door frame. "I bet it would work better than a shower."

Marley was shaking her head before he got out the words. "I don't think—"

"You could wear a bathing suit," he said, removing all the obstacles.

"No, I—"

"You could get in the tub all by yourself," he continued, although that wasn't his preference.

"No, thank—"

"I would bring you home and not try to talk you into staying all night." He hesitated, then modified the offer. "Tonight."

Marley took a quick breath. Her gaze deepened. "Your offer is very generous," she said in a soft, unsteady voice. "But I think not."

"Why not?" he asked. "Do I make you nervous?"

"Not really," she said quickly, then sighed. "A little," she confessed.

His heart pounded harder at the expression on her face. "You make me a little nervous, too."

"Me?" she asked in shocked disbelief.

He lifted his hand to rub his knuckles over her cheek. "Yeah, you. Why are you surprised?"

She licked her lips and her eyelids fluttered. "Well, I thought we had already talked about this. I'm not really your type."

"Uh-huh," he said, stroking her skin and looking at her pink lips. "Maybe my type is changing."

Her eyes widened and she backed away. "No, it isn't."

She looked so endearingly panicked that he smiled. "How do you know?"

She blinked. "I just do. I just know it." She paused, then laughed nervously. Still holding his gaze, she pulled her key from her pocket and groped behind her. "I read minds. Didn't I tell you that?"

"No, you didn't."

"Well, I do. In fact I can read your mind right now and I know exactly what you want."

He was in deep trouble if she was telling the truth, because he wanted her in his Jacuzzi and out of her clothes. He stepped closer. "What's that?"

She pulled something from behind her back and thrust it at him. "A tarantula." She smiled and pushed open her door. "Thanks for the ride. I'll give you a call tomorrow after I get a chance to look at these records. G'night."

"Marley," he said in a quiet voice.

She paused, tense and uneasy in the doorway. No more pushing tonight, he decided. "Thanks for the spider."

She let out a long breath of relief. "You're welcome. Good night, Joe."

He watched her close the door and stared at it for a long moment. Joe wanted to see if Marley truly rocked his world or if his imagination was running away with him. He had a strange premonition about this woman. He wasn't sure about her at all. But this was sure, he was going to want more from her than Tootsie Rolls and plastic tarantulas.

Four

"Sam has his hands full with those boys," Marley told Joe the next day as he stood in her den. Although she'd told him they could handle the rest of her consultation over the phone, he'd insisted on coming over. There he stood, like a big tree growing out of her floor. Unavoidable.

Still rattled from his offer last night, she was determined to get him out the door as soon as possible. Then she could breathe normally. Then she could *think* normally.

"I checked over the individual histories last night, and what you've got is a group of very bright high-achievers. The regular camp plan is probably not going to work. These boys need to be challenged. Since you want them to work together cohesively, you might try a joint project where they have to cooperate with each other to achieve the goal...."

"Smart kids?" Joe said in disbelief. "That's all it is. We've got a bunch of smart kids."

"That pretty much sums it up. I can give Sam a few pointers, but he's already doing a lot right."

Joe shook his head. "If this was so easy, then why didn't we see it?"

After all of Joe's taunts about her profession, Marley couldn't resist sliding one in of her own. "Because you're not a trained shrink. We occasionally provide a useful service."

"I never denied your usefulness," he said in a velvet tone that made her think of the dream she'd tried to forget.

Marley's stomach dipped. Oops. In over her head again. She stood and handed him the paperwork. "Well, that's the gist of it. Sam can give me a call, and I'll be glad to talk to him. The main task will be coming up with a project." She shrugged when he continued to stand in front of her. "So I guess this wraps things up."

He stepped closer and cocked his head to one side. "Some things," he said. "Not everything."

Marley felt a thread of uneasiness. "What else, then?" she asked, though she wasn't sure she wanted to know.

"There's something between you and me," he said bluntly. "Damned if I know what it is, but I want to find out."

Marley's heart stuttered. "I thought we already

went over this. I'm not your type," she reminded him.

"This isn't about types." He moved close enough that she could feel his heat, smell his scent and read the intent in his eyes.

"This is about you and me, Marley."

She took a careful breath. "I...I don't get involved with clients or—"

"I'm not a client. I'm not paying. Remember?"

Oh, Lord, her heart was pounding so hard she feared she might pass out.

"You're not denying it, are you?"

She swallowed. "Denying what?"

"That there's something between us. Something different."

Yes, yes, yes. "No," she said, the truth popping out. She barely resisted the urge to pace. "But I think it's a chemical thing and not something we could base a long-term relationship on, so—"

"Whoa." Joe took her hand. "I didn't—" He looked down at her hand, then back at her face. "You're trembling."

Marley didn't breathe.

"Don't worry. I'm not talking about forever, Marley." He slid his fingers through hers, and the gesture somehow felt sexual, intimate.

"We're curious about each other, so let's satisfy our curiosity."

"And how do you think we should do that?"

"The usual way. Spend time with each other," he told her in a voice that slid under her skin. "And see what happens."

A ripple of anticipation ran down her spine. "That sounds like a gambler talking," she whispered.

"You can't win if you don't play."

"But you can lose," Marley pointed out.

"What? What can you lose except a little time?" She swallowed. "Your heart."

He laughed wryly. "You gotta have a heart before you can lose it. I'm the tin man, remember."

Marley shook her head. "I'm not."

"Maybe you're Dorothy, and you're going to lead me to Oz."

She closed her eyes and laughed. "If this is a line, it's the most original one I've heard."

"I haven't been accused of using lines on women."

"You didn't need them," Marley concluded.

He shrugged. "I never promise what I can't deliver."

He was so confident, so totally sure of himself, that despite her reticence he almost *demanded* she meet his challenge. "Okay, Mr. Tin Man, exactly what *can* you deliver?"

"I'm brutally honest. I won't try to take over your life. I play fair."

Marley looked into his dark eyes and disagreed. "That's a matter of opinion."

He gave a slow grin. "Okay. If I decide not to play fair, I can make you like it."

"This may not be a good idea," Marley said as she allowed herself to be dragged to Lynn's hairstylist. Her G.T.A. had grilled her nonstop about Joe.

Heaven help her, Lynn had then taken it upon herself to aid Marley in a "makeover." Marley looked at Lynn's asymmetrical haircut and six pierced earrings in one ear and the little hoop in her eyebrow. She didn't want to know if there were any other piercings.

"It's a great idea," Lynn corrected, looking at Marley and shaking her head. "You need an update in every way."

"Thanks for the affirmation."

"Oh, stop," Lynn said. "You've got the basic equipment. You just need some work on the options if you're going to be the main squeeze of one of Denver's top-ten eligible bachelors."

"Main squeeze," Marley echoed, sinking into a chair in the waiting area of the funky salon. "Denver's top-ten?"

"Yep. I recognized him from his photo when he walked into your office."

Marley felt a strange sinking sensation inside her again. She was in over her head with this man. "This is crazy," she whispered. "My stomach feels like I'm going up the down elevator. My throat is tight, my muscles tense. All my body signals indicate that I—"

"—am chicken," Lynn said, and Marley thought her G.T.A. could use a little refinement of her communication skills.

"You're just not used to being involved with a man like Joe." Lynn gave a little moan and fanned herself. "Most of us aren't used to being involved with a man like Joe. You've been around preadolescent males too long.''

"You sound like my father. There are advantages to working with kids. Appearances aren't as important. The games they play tend to come in boxes.''

Lynn gave Marley an impish grin. "Growing up's hell, isn't it?''

"You don't understand,'' Marley said. "I'm used to men who are more—'' She searched for the right word.

Lynn raised her eyebrows. *"More? More how?''*

Marley concentrated. "Well, maybe I didn't mean *more.* Maybe I meant I'm used to men who are less—''

"Now *that* I can understand,'' Lynn interjected with a firm nod. "I can understand how you would be used to men who are less, because Joe is definitely *more* in all the right ways.''

Marley sighed. "I think he has a practice of moving faster than I do.''

"And I bet he didn't need to practice much to be perfect.''

Marley groaned. "Lynn.''

"You can tell he's good at sex,'' Lynn continued, undeterred by Marley's tone. "You can tell it by the way he walks, the way he talks and the way he looks at you. If he wore a sign, it would say Caution— Flammable.''

"Stop,'' Marley said, irritated because the same thoughts had run through her mind.

"He's the kind of man who will get you out of

your clothes so fast it'll make your head spin. But he'll make you feel so good you won't care.''

Marley felt the surface of her skin heat as if she'd just drunk two glasses of wine. She was trying to keep her strong attraction to Joe under control, to take her time. *Physician, heal thyself,* she tried to tell herself, but felt as if she'd been strapped into a rocket ship, and communication with Houston was impossible.

"Dr. Marley," Lynn said, "my mother says many men may pass through a woman's life, but it's a very rare man who reminds you that you're a woman and makes you damn glad of it. A wise woman doesn't pass up that man." Blinking at Lynn's words of wisdom, Marley took a deep breath and produced a litany of mental disputes. She opened her mouth.

"Marley Fuller," a woman said as she walked into the waiting area. "I'm ready for you."

Stalled, Marley stared at the hairstylist. She managed a smile, but strongly considered running. The stylist had teal hair.

"Scrunch, don't brush. Scrunch, don't brush," Marley repeated the hairstylist's words as she scrunched, then reached for her brush. Joe had invited her to dinner at his house. He'd promised candlelight and vegetables, but she hadn't thought this was a good idea from the get-go.

Pulling her hair into a ponytail, she stopped staring at the stranger in the mirror, grabbed a washcloth and headed for the phone. Snatching Joe's list of telephone numbers from the magnet on her refrigerator, she punched out the first one and waited for his voice mail to kick in. "Hi, this is Marley. It's a beautiful day, so I was wondering if you'd mind a little change in plans. If you get off early enough, we could take a bike ride and have a little picnic.

"Let me know if that sounds good to you," she said as she rubbed the makeup off her face. She hung up, then punched out the next number on the list.

Three hours later Joe joined Marley in pedaling up one of the back roads close to her house. Thus far, the major benefit to this outing was that by allowing her to lead, he was treated to an uninterrupted view of her rear end. The side effect to his view was that he wanted to pull that gorgeous rear end against his swollen crotch and persuade her to let him make love to her. Joe had this driving sense that if he could get inside Marley, inside her body, inside her head, that he'd be satisfied—the crazy inexplicable wanting that nagged him would then go away.

"Easy, bud," he muttered to himself. "The lady's still jittery." This was an unusual date for Joe, but Marley was proving she was an unusual woman. Except for sculpting their bodies to perfection, most women he'd dated hadn't been interested in physical activity unless it involved the exercise of acquiring clothes or jewelry.

"Okay to stop here?" Marley called over her shoulder.

He glanced at the small clearing up ahead. "Fine with me," Joe said, coasting to her side and dismounting his bike. She wobbled as she got off her bike and he automatically reached out to steady her.

"Altitude still bothering you?" he asked, rubbing his hands over the soft, warm skin of her upper arms.

"It must be," she said under her breath, her gaze meeting his.

It was the most natural thing in the world to slide his hand down her back and draw her against him. He skimmed a finger over her pink nose. "You burn easily."

"It's not nice to rub it in," she said, surprising him when she didn't move away.

He nuzzled her hair. "You remind me of a daffodil. Aren't they one of the first spring flowers to bloom? Back East, I remember sometimes even seeing them before the final snow of the season. Pretty flowers with snow on them." Geez, where had that semipoetic thought come from? He took a quick breath. "What do I smell?"

"Soap, shampoo." She gave a helpless grin. "Deodorant?"

He shook his head and chuckled. "No French perfume, huh?"

"Nope, just me," she said, her face growing solemn as he dipped his head.

"Just you is enough," he murmured, and took her mouth. Tasting her sigh and rolling his lips leisurely over hers, he knew he'd waited entirely too long to kiss her, to hold her, to have her. He felt the brush of her nipples on his chest and stifled a groan.

Her body melded with his, and he slid his leg between her thighs, wanting to caress her. The little hint of a shiver that ran through her drove him wild.

Hungry, he opened his mouth and devoured her.

He used his hands to learn her shape. He skimmed over her hips, measured the sweet indention of her waist and counted her ribs with his fingers. Brushing the bottom of her full breast with the back of his hand, he felt the soft sound she made, and it caught at his heart, the heart he'd thought didn't exist.

He drew back, and she automatically leaned toward him, her hands catching on his chest. "Oh, my-y-y-y-y," she said, taking deep breaths.

She didn't even try to hide her reaction, and he felt that same tugging again in his chest. He could have her, he thought, taking a few deep breaths of his own. "You sure you don't want to go back to my house?"

She shook her head and covered her eyes. "You should move," she said, yet still clung to him. "I can't think straight with you standing so close."

He liked the way she felt in his arms, softness and strength. Still sensing her resistance, however, he wondered how it would be when she stopped balking at what was happening between them. He wondered how it would be when she let him take her fully.

His gut tightened at the thought, and he stroked her cheek. "I learned a long time ago that thinking too much can get in your way."

"And I learned that thinking can keep you out of trouble," she told him, and he sighed as she pulled slightly away.

"Trouble's not all bad," he told her, leaning down and brushing his mouth over her ear. "In fact, I think you haven't gotten into enough trouble, Marley."

Later, after they'd eaten vegetarian pitas with bean

sprouts and ridden home, Joe stole a good-night kiss, but still didn't succeed in coaxing her to visit his house.

It was turning into a turf war, he thought with a scowl as he pulled into his driveway. Glancing at the three-story contemporary structure, he was reminded again that he had made it. He had reached his goal.

One of his few indulgences, the house wasn't as ostentatious as Graceland, but Joe still often felt as if he didn't belong there. Parking his Suburban in the three-car garage, he entered the mudroom and walked across the gleaming tile floors of the large, well-equipped, but seldom-used kitchen. Polished copper pots hung from above the center island. If not for the scrupulous attention of his cleaning lady, they would be coated with dust, again, from lack of use. His footsteps echoed hollowly as he made his way through the ground floor.

Decorated to perfection in subtle earth tones, the leather furniture, lush Persian wool carpet and imported fixtures and accessories evoked an image of luxury.

But Joe found little comfort in it.

Floor-to-ceiling windows exposed a generous amount of sunlight in both the afternoon and evening, and with the flick of his finger on a remote control, he could start a fire in one of the three gas fireplaces.

But Joe found little warmth in it. His golden retriever, Dixie, ambled toward him and nuzzled his hand with her wet nose. Joe petted and made a fuss over her.

Tail wagging, his dog followed him up the curving staircase to the master bedroom on the second floor. Joe ditched his shoes, grabbed a beer from the mini-bar, then strode past the king-size bed and master bath to the spiral staircase that led to his favorite place in the house.

He had paid through the nose for the magnificent view from his roof-top balcony. During the day he could see the Rockies in their jagged splendor. At night the stars looked close enough to touch, and the breeze washed over him in a familiar way. Standing here gave him an odd, but sweet, sense of nostalgia for his childhood days spent in the Bad Boys' tree house.

Joe had spent most of his life not belonging, but he had almost belonged then. His house, his huge, exclusive, exquisite house reminded him that he had made it to the other side. He didn't have to ride his bike from his shabby apartment to get to Cherry Lane anymore. Hell, he'd made it way past Cherry Lane.

He glanced down the spiral stairs, and a gnawing emptiness dragged at him again. It should be enough, he thought, swearing under his breath. He was alone.

He'd thought he preferred solitude, but lately, more and more that wasn't true. He wanted real warmth in his life, human sunshine in his home. His mind turned to Marley as it often did lately. She was more authentic than any woman he'd ever met. He wondered how his house would feel with her presence.

She was light and energy, laughter and heart. He wanted her. He wanted her light and laughter all for himself. It was an incredibly selfish desire, he thought, but she drew him, and Joe had the strange sense that she could give him what he needed.

She was struggling with it, but she wanted his passion. He could read it on her face and feel it in her body. It would be an even trade, he thought, when they finally made love, because his passion for her was growing to rival the vastness of the Rockies. The knowledge brought him no comfort, but it made him determined. Joe wanted Marley, and it was a fact that it might take a while, but Joe always got what he wanted.

"I can't tell who you're trying to torment more," Marley said as she joined him for dinner at one of his restaurants. "Your employees or me."

He grinned slightly, enjoying the way her eyes sparkled in the candlelight. "I'm not tormenting anyone," he told her. "We're just having dinner."

"Uh-huh," she said, her voice dripping with disbelief. "Then why do your waiters continue to try to persuade me to eat steak?"

"Because it's a steak restaurant, and they want to sell you on our superior specialty."

"And they work extra hard to convert me because I'm with you."

Joe thought of the other women who had joined him for dinner here. "Well," he admitted, "you are the first vegetarian."

She laughed, and the full sound rippled through him. "You make *vegetarian* sound like alien."

He grinned. "Your words." He narrowed his gaze,

looking at her, trying to nail what was different. "What's different about your hair?"

Marley rolled her eyes. "I got it cut. I'm supposed to scrunch instead of brush, and I haven't mastered the technique."

"I like it. It looks like you just—" He broke off when he saw the color rise in her cheeks, then leaned forward. "What did you think I was going to say?"

Her blush deepened, and she stared at him as if she was lost.

"You're blushing."

Marley closed her eyes, the sensual tone of his voice sending her tumbling again. "It's kind of you to point that out."

He laughed, the sexy, rumbling sound vibrating through her. "C'mon, Marley, answer my question. What did you think I was going to say?"

Marley opened her eyes and glared at him. It was ridiculous to feel so embarrassed, but whenever she was with Joe, she felt a little too bare, as if he could read her more easily than she preferred. She took a careful breath. "I thought you were going to say my hair looks like I just had sex."

"For a psychologist, you seem to get tense about discussing sex."

"When it involves me it becomes more personal," she told him. "My emotions get involved, and I have strong feelings and thoughts about having sex. I think many people have sex without their minds and feelings fully engaged, and it ends up being *junk* sex. For me, I want sex to be much more than two bodies together."

"Passion," Joe said, and she saw glints of the same in his eyes.

"Yes, and emotion."

A long silence followed. He held her gaze, and she felt the cord of something powerful connecting her to him.

"I agree," he finally said, and her heart clenched at the absolute determination on his face. If his eyes could talk, they would say, *I'm going to have you.*

Five

Marley's mouth went dry at the force of raw desire Joe emanated. She was peripherally aware of the muted voices of other restaurant patrons and the clink of silverware and plates, but Joe commanded her attention. The ease with which he held her disturbed her, and she tried in vain to think of a way to break the spell.

"Joe Caruthers!" A woman's voice blessedly shattered the moment.

Marley watched his eye briefly twitch as he turned his head toward the middle-aged woman practically tripping over herself to reach their table.

"Janine Perkins," he muttered under his breath, but stood.

"I'm so glad to catch you," she gushed. "I've left numerous messages on your answering machine about our dinner honoring Denver's Men of the Year. You do intend to join us, don't you?''

Joe gave an apologetic shrug. "I'm not sure I can make it, Janine. I'm acquiring another franchise in Wyoming, and that could wreck my schedule. Marley,'' he said, turning to her, looking as if he'd rather eat fish scales, "this is Janine Perkins. She's very active in Denver's civic organizations.''

Marley nodded and smiled. "It's nice to meet you, Ms. Perkins. I'm new to the area. What's this about Denver's Men of the Year?''

"It's a very high honor," Ms. Perkins said, her voice quavering with enthusiasm. "We honor women at a separate luncheon. The major civic organizations nominate and vote for the top three men who have made a positive impact on our community. This year Joe will be honored because of his fabulous summer camp for boys at risk, his program of hiring welfare recipients who are trying to improve their lives by attending college or trade school and his financial support of our home for unwed mothers.''

Marley was impressed—surprised and not surprised at the same time. She glanced at Joe. He now looked as if he had eaten those fish scales. She smiled. "Denver's proud of you."

He shot her a dark look, then turned back to Ms. Perkins. "I'm honored, but I'll have to look at my schedule again.''

"You *will* try to work us in, won't you?" Ms. Perkins asked, twisting her fingers together. Marley would bet Janine knew Joe was his own man and would do what he darn well pleased. "The civic organizations of Denver are counting on you."

"I appreciate it, and I'll do what I can," he said, and Marley saw the twitch again.

"Thank you," Ms. Perkins solemnly said, taking his hand, then nodding at Marley. "It was nice meeting you."

As the woman left, Joe sank into his chair with a sigh. "God help me."

Marley choked back a snicker. "Is it that bad? You've done these terrific things and—"

He held up his hand. "Let's stop right there. First, I haven't done anything terrific except throw some green around."

"That's not true. You hire people trying to get off welfare," she pointed out.

"Which will ultimately reduce some of the huge sucking sound I hear every time I pay my IRS bill. They get off welfare and get better jobs," he said, pointing to his chest, "I benefit, too."

Marley leaned back in her seat. "And the donations to the home for unwed mothers?"

"Tax deduction, plus the teenage girls who get involved with this home are less likely to repeat the unwed experience."

Marley nodded. "Uh-huh. So the only reason you do all this is because you will ultimately benefit. Right?"

"Right," he said shortly, looking away.

This time Marley let the silence fall between them. She could understand why the award would bother him. He was a private man. She wondered why, however, he was so determined not to accept the simple goodness of his gestures.

"You're such a fraud," she finally said.

He jerked back to stare at her. "A *fraud?*" he asked, but it sounded much more like a demand.

"Yes, a fraud. You can't accept that you *are* motivated to do some good with the money and power you've gained. You're determined to give off this attitude that you don't care and everything you do is for the sake of the great American dollar."

"It has been," he insisted. "And if the damn civic league wants to honor me, let them honor my camp with dead presidents."

"Dead presidents?" Marley echoed.

"Money," he practically snarled.

Uncowed, she shook her head. "It's still a matter of choice. You could be like Scrooge and hoard all your money. You're using it to improve other people's lives."

"Tax deductions."

"Bull," she returned, seeing surprise, frustration and a tiny flicker of admiration in his brooding brown eyes. "The tax excuse is just a cover-up. You're a good man. Deal with it. I can understand why you would be uncomfortable with the honor, but did you ever think it was just their way of saying thank you?"

"I've been to a few of these before to drum up some money for the camp, and they're boring as hell."

Marley laughed lightly. "Oh, I'm surprised at you. You're an incredibly fascinating, creative man. I find it difficult to believe you couldn't find a way to make this more interesting for you.''

She saw the grudging challenge in his set chin. He slit his eyes at her. ''Have you always had a Pollyanna complex about finding the good in everybody?''

She laughed again. ''Nice try for a diversion, but it won't work. I just don't have a hang-up about money.''

''Everybody has a hang-up about money,'' he muttered, ''especially if they don't have any. So, what's your hang-up?'' he asked, curiosity threading through his tone. ''Let me guess,'' he said, lowering his voice. ''Sex.''

Marley's stomach dipped at the energy zipping between them. How had he turned the conversation on her? ''I wouldn't call it a hang-up.''

He lifted his eyebrows. ''Then what would you call it?''

''I would call my attitude cautious,'' she said slowly, choosing her words with care and forcing herself to meet his gaze. ''Particular.''

He studied her, then nodded. ''Okay. Then how would you like to help me with my hang-up?''

Confused, she shrugged. ''I don't do adult therapy. Actually, I don't do any therapy any—''

He slid his hand over hers, stopping her midsyllable. His slightly callused hand swallowed hers, and Marley feared it would require all her will to prevent him from swallowing her heart as easily.

''I'm not talking therapy or even money, really. I'm talking about my hang-up about going to this boring award dinner. If you went with me, then I don't think I would be bored.''

Marley felt that dipping sensation again and struggled with an urge to backpedal. "I'll have to check my calendar.''

"Lame, lame, lame," he said with a bad grin.

She bit her lip. "Well, I do have other commitments.''

"And if you're free that night?''

She felt trapped.

"C'mon, Marley, having you there will make it bearable," he said, lacing his fingers through hers.

She sighed. "Is it formal?''

"Yep," he said, smiling cheerlessly.

"I hate formal affairs. I always spill something.''

"Now you know why I don't want to go.''

But she thought it might be good for Joe to hear his good deeds recognized. Beneath his capitalist bravado beat a sensitive heart. "Okay. Let's go, and the deal is we do whatever is necessary to have a good time.''

"Whatever?" he repeated, his tone deepening to a dangerous velvet softness. "We do *whatever* is necessary to have a good time?''

"As long as it's legal," she said, feeling a twinge of trepidation. "And doesn't hurt anyone.''

"In that case," he said, smiling like a wolf, "I think the best way to have a good time is to help you with your hang-up.''

Joe showed up at her office nearly every day just as Marley was ready to leave. He was becoming a habit. She wasn't certain he was a *good* habit, but being with him felt good.

He touched her naturally, as if it wasn't only his desire but also his right. She could have argued with that attitude if he didn't constantly encourage her to treat him the same way. He didn't hide the fact that he wanted to make love with her, and she sensed he would have pushed her if he thought it would work. He had no idea how close she was to going straight over the edge.

The strong, rational side kept her from going to his house. Marley could tell he wanted her there, but she resisted. It was easy to explain even to herself, but she didn't want to be like the other women who had passed through his life. It had become important to her to enrich him in a way that had nothing to do with his money.

He had already given her the gift of a deeper appreciation for her femininity.

On the other hand, she had introduced him to the world of bean sprouts. Something told her, however, that the bean sprouts hadn't knocked his socks off.

At her dinner table, Joe downed the last swallow of his beer after he finished the meal she'd prepared. "You want to tell me one more time what I just ate?"

Marley's lips twitched. "A vegetarian pita."

"With beans, vegetables, cheese and—" he smiled grimly "—bean sprouts."

"I'll leave them off yours next time if you'd like," she offered, and rose to take her plate to the sink.

Joining her with his own, he looked relieved.

"Thank you. They remind me of weeds. Now that we've finished dinner, it's time for my surprise."

Marley fought a wave of wariness as she loaded the few dishes into the dishwasher. "I was hoping for some hints."

"We have to drive to get there. You'll need to climb steps, and based on what you've told me you'll like it."

Curious, she glanced at him. "How far do we drive? What will I like about it?"

"Not far," he said and kissed her on the nose. "No more hints."

Glancing down the length of her sleeveless sundress, he skimmed his finger down her arm. "You'll need a sweater."

"It's chilly where we're going?"

His gaze was obscure. "It's often chilly at night in Colorado."

She sighed. "You're being vague."

"You're procrastinating."

She groaned, but smiled. There were many things about their relationship that were reciprocal. He didn't let her get away with much, and she didn't let him get away with anything, either.

After running to her bedroom to grab the sweater, she walked with him out to his Suburban. She glanced up at the stars. "Beautiful night," she murmured as she slid into the passenger seat.

"Uh-huh," he said, but he was looking at her.

A few miles down the road he stopped the car and pulled to the side. He pulled out a handkerchief. "To protect the secrecy of our destination, I'll have to ask you to wear this.''

Marley blinked at the makeshift blindfold. "You're joking?"

He shook his head. "I promised a surprise."

She gave him a doubtful look. "I wouldn't do this for everyone."

"I know," he said as he tied the handkerchief behind her head. "And you won't regret it." She felt his breath just before his lips meshed with hers. His tongue made a sensual invasion. She was blind, but she saw a kaleidoscope of colors. She was sitting perfectly still, but she would have sworn she was spinning.

Marley couldn't see Joe, yet she felt him, as she had in her dream, inside her. The sensations rushing through her were so strong she shivered. He must have felt it.

"Cold?" he murmured, rubbing her arms.

Marley hesitated, wondering how the truth would affect him. "No," she managed, taking a step closer to the edge of the cliff.

"No?"

She swallowed. "Sometimes you make me tremble."

His hands stopped their soothing movement, and she thought she should have done this when she could *see* him, when she could read his face. Her stomach tightened as the silence grew between them. She was just about to reach up and push aside the handkerchief, when she felt his fingers on either side of her jaw.

His lips touched hers again, and this time, she sensed, he wanted to show instead of tell. His mouth was tender and possessive, his tongue stroking, simulating a deeper joining. One step further and he would be touching her swollen breasts. One step further and their clothes would be gone, and she would be stroking his hardness. One step further and he would be inside her.

He made love to her mouth, and when he finally pulled away, she struggled with tears. He made her feel so much.

His breath labored, he swore under his breath. "At this rate, it's gonna take all night to get there."

"Can't have that," she managed in a shaky voice. Groping for the button to lower the power windows, she finally found it and turned her face to the cool night air.

His hand covered hers, and her fluttering ceased. "Marley," he said.

She took a deep breath. "Yes?"

"You okay?"

Lie, she told herself. "I will be," she said.

He pressed his mouth to her palm. "We'll be there before you know it."

He was right. Just moments passed before Joe was leading her through an area that smelled vaguely of oil and car exhaust, then through a door. Her footsteps were loud on the tile floor. She heard the scrape of an animal's footsteps and felt a cold nose nudging at her hand.

Her stomach flipped over. "You brought me to your house."

His hand tightened slightly. "We haven't arrived yet."

Marley tensed with mixed feelings. She'd grown curious about seeing where Joe lived, but she'd also had a strange resistance to being here where other women had been, too.

"More steps," he warned her. "Dixie, back off," he muttered to the dog when Marley nearly tripped over the canine.

She reached out to touch the dog's silky fur. "Golden retriever or Irish setter?"

"Golden retriever. Setters can be high-strung."

Marley thought she could be, too, as she allowed him to lead her upstairs. She was sorely tempted to pull off the handkerchief.

"Not yet," he said as if he'd read her mind.

Following him inside another door, she felt thick carpet cushion her feet. The scent of this room was masculine and familiar. It smelled like Joe.

Her heart beat faster. She cleared her throat. "This is your bedroom?"

"We haven't reached our destination," he told her.

"You didn't answer me."

He hesitated. "What makes you say that?"

She hesitated. "It smells like you."

He stopped, and she couldn't see the emotions shimmering inside him. But she could feel them.

He swore under his breath and muttered, "Dangerous."

"More steps," he told her. "These will be tougher. We'll go slowly."

Marley clung to the curved wooden rail and Joe's strong hand. Her feet kept bumping into the narrow steps, and she realized what she was navigating. "A spiral staircase," she murmured, surprised. "Where are we going?"

"Almost there."

Again he was as good as his word, and Marley stood on a solid flat platform. The wind whipped through her hair, and she felt the lack of light. Was she outside? "What...where—"

Joe removed the blindfold. "You said part of the reason you moved to Colorado was because you loved a great view."

Marley stared at the velvet blanket of sparkling stars. Overwhelmed by the beautiful sight, she shook her head. "They look close enough to touch," she whispered, and turned to Joe.

He wasn't looking at the stars. He was watching her. Thumbs hooked in his pockets, he was waiting, assessing.

Almost nervous, she thought, then quickly dismissed the notion. She'd never made a man nervous in her life.

"You like it?" he finally asked with a shrug.

Something inside her broke free, and she flew into his arms. He felt warm and strong. "It's beautiful! I feel like you gave me a gift."

Stunned for a moment, he chuckled, then held her against him. "I guess this means you like it."

"Like it!" She pulled back to look at him. "What I want to know is how you make yourself go to work each day. I would be hard-pressed not to play hooky all the time.''

''Hey, even a capitalist has to pay his light bill,'' he told her.

She glanced up at the sky again, and chill bumps rose on her skin. The horizon stretched wide, giving her a sense of space and contentment. ''You don't have to pay for these lights.''

''True,'' he said of the stars. ''This is my favorite part of the house. When I was a kid, I was in a club and we met in a tree house. I remember how much I liked being up high, able to see.''

''Have you ever gone back?''

He shook his head. ''I got a wedding invitation from one of the guys in the club last year, and I sent a gift.''

''You think they would have rather had you?''

He met her gaze. ''Maybe. What about you?''

Her heart dipped. ''What about me?'' she echoed.

''Yeah.'' He lowered his head and slid his leg between hers. ''Would you like to have me?'' He skimmed his fingertips up her ribs to the underside of her breast. ''Play hooky with me.''

Six

He felt so good, so right, and Marley, who had always relied on her eminently reasonable mind, slipped further away from reason. She closed her eyes to the magic of the night, but that only heightened her awareness of his musky scent and the warm strength of his body. His muscular chest abraded her sensitive nipples, and his powerful thigh slid between hers, making her want to feel his bare skin against hers, making her want him as close as he could get.

"I can't figure out," he muttered as he rubbed his mouth from side to side over hers, "how you do this to me."

"Do what?" Marley managed, clinging to his shoulders.

"Make me *lose* it," he told her, and made a sound between a growl and groan that put a coil in her nether regions. Taking her mouth, he pulled up her dress and slid his hands underneath to her bare thighs.

Marley couldn't breathe.

"I want to take this dress off of you," he said, "and get to know every inch of you inside and out. And when I'm done, I want to start all over again."

Marley closed her eyes. "Oh, Joe, it's too soon."

"No, it isn't. It wouldn't have been too soon if we'd made love that first night we met."

Marley sucked in a quick breath and opened her eyes to gape at him. "We'd never even laid eyes on each other before."

"There was something between us even then."

His eyes, even more than his words, wouldn't allow her to deny it.

"You know it, too, don't you?"

Marley turned her head into his shoulder. If she didn't admit it aloud, she might have a smidgen of protection left.

"Can you tell I want to make love to you?" he asked, sliding his hands dangerously closer to her femininity, stroking the outside of her silk panties.

She bit her lip to keep from moaning.

"Can you tell how much I want to touch you?" He slipped his fingers past the sheer barrier and found her.

He gently caressed her, worrying the tiny nub of sensation until she was trembling, and a soft mingling of distress and pleasure bubbled from her throat.

"Do you know I want to hold your breasts in my

hands?'' he told, more than asked her. "That I want to put them in my mouth and taste you?"

She wanted more. Her heart, her body, wanted more. She strained against him, and reading her body like a book, he plunged his finger inside her.

The tightness within her burst open, pleasure tearing through her at breakneck speed. Gasping, Marley jerked in surprise.

"I want to be in you, Marley. Let me in. Play hooky with me," he told her, pushing her panties so they slid to her ankles. "Just for one day."

Just for one day. Temporary. Joe wasn't interested in anything long lasting. The reality seeped into her mind. She came to earth with a hard, bone-jarring thud. Shaking her head, she pushed away, though she was still trembling. Oh, Lord, she hoped she wouldn't fall. She fought a terrible burning sensation in her eyes. She struggled with the need to give him everything she had.

"I can't do one day," she managed, still shaking her head. "I'm not a one-day woman."

That night Marley couldn't go to sleep when she went to bed. Too stirred up emotionally, physically, she left her bed, pulled open the curtains of her bedroom window and stared at the stars. Filled to overflowing with thoughts of Joe, she searched for a practical answer to all she was feeling, but she suspected there was no easy, practical solution.

She was struck with a sense of fate as bright and as unavoidable as the stars she was watching. The deep knowledge sank inside her that somehow, some way, she was destined to be connected with Joe. It caught her off guard, because she'd never felt this way about a man before. Plus, she had too many practical objections why she couldn't be involved with him.

She listed them in her mind. He had too many past relationships with women. Past behavior was a predictor of future practice, which meant her relationship with him was likely to have the half-life of a stalk of celery. He was also not inclined toward commitment. He was more ruthless than compassionate, moody and not easily manageable. He was not the kind of man to take home to Mom *or* Dad. Plus, she and Joe didn't share the same values or priorities about life.

That should settle it, she thought. Finished, kaput, the end.

There were, however, too many layers to Joe Caruthers to put him in a nice, neat, don't-touch package. Marley saw past the toughness to the tenderness, and his moodiness showed a range of emotion that excited her. He challenged her. He stretched her. He made her look at herself in a different way. He made her appreciate her womanhood. He wanted her.

Practical or not, she wanted him, too.

She glanced up at the stars, searching for answers. The insistent sense of fate remained, and she wondered if she could fight it.

The next morning Marley awakened, wondering if Joe would give up on her now. She suspected he wasn't accustomed to being turned down. As she rose from her bed, her stomach sank to her knees. She didn't want to miss knowing him, being with him. Facing her bathroom mirror, she scowled at her extreme reaction.

She hadn't been man crazy since high school, and she wasn't the least bit interested in repeating the insanity. She took a shower and sudsed her hair, humming a tune from an old musical about washing a man out of her hair.

Her doorbell rang just as she stepped out of the shower, and she threw on her robe. "Just a minute," she called.

She opened the door to Joe. In his hands she saw a white bag and two cups of coffee. In his eyes she saw a heart-stopping determination.

"Thought you might like a pastry and coffee this morning," he said, moving past her. She felt a dart of dry amusement at his assumption that he was welcome. He had an incredible sense of personal power, and it wasn't misplaced.

"Your timing's amazing," she said, closing the door and slowly joining him in her sunny kitchen.

He shrugged, unloading pastries dusted in powdered sugar. "How'd you sleep last night?" he asked in a casual tone.

Marley paused. "The sandman was on vacation."

He raised a dark eyebrow. "He skipped my house, too. I thought you could use some coffee," he told her, and sat down.

She shook her head and smiled. "I'm still amazed at your timing."

"Don't be." He narrowed his eyes. "There's

something between you and me. Strange as hell, but it's there. If I were a New Age type, I'd call it energy."

Her heart thumped crazily in her chest. "I'm assuming that means you're not New Age. So what do you call it?"

He frowned. "I'm a man, and I like simple explanations. Normally I would say it's lust. Sex," he added with a shrug. "That's part of it. But there's more."

"More," she echoed over the lump in her throat.

He nodded and wiggled his finger for her to come closer. "Come here."

Wary, Marley took a step toward him. "Why?"

"We need to talk," he said, and before she could tell him she could talk better at ninety paces, he snagged her arm and pulled her onto his lap.

He tore off a bite of the powdery pastry and lifted it to her lips. "Here," he said, and slipped his arm securely around her waist. "You smell good."

Feeling deliciously surrounded by him, Marley relaxed a fraction. "Thank you," she murmured, then opened her mouth to taste the pastry. "Umm."

Joe began to rub his hand back and forth over her stomach in a soothing motion. "I don't want you to get tense, but there's something you need to know."

Her heart hammered against her rib cage, and she felt light-headed, but his gentle massage and the low tone of his voice lulled her. "What's that?"

"I want you like I've never wanted another woman."

His words rocked her, but the reassuring tone he

used kept her from walking up her kitchen wall. "It'll pass," she managed, and he fed her another bite of the pastry.

"No," he said, nuzzling her neck. "But that's okay, because I'm gonna get you, Marley."

Again the words were at odds with his voice, and she felt a shiver run through her. His hand skimmed the underside of her breasts. She swallowed the bite. "I'm not sure you ought to do that. You might not know what to do with me once you get me."

He gave a rough chuckle. "I know what to do, and part of my goal is to make sure you like it."

Marley felt a rush of arousal spanning from her mouth to the tips of her breasts, between her thighs all the way to her toes. "Too soon," she said over the lump in her throat. "I'm not ready."

"I can help with that." He lowered his mouth to hers and licked the powdered sugar from her lips.

She inched her fingers up his arms to hold on. He skimmed his mouth and tongue over hers, tasting her, clouding her mind with her want for him. It was the most erotic experience for him to eat her as if she were a delicacy he wanted to both devour and savor.

Sighing, Marley gave herself over to the sensations. She opened her mouth and bowed to her own hunger for him, steeping her senses in his scent and taste. She grew hot under his touch.

He shifted her slightly and lowered his mouth to her throat where her pulse beat frantically. "You're not wearing anything under this robe, are you?"

His hands skimmed over her breasts and she felt her nipples harden against the terry cloth covering them. "No," she said, and the little word surprised her by sounding like a moan of sexual need.

Still nuzzling her neck, he brushed the robe down her shoulders, baring her breasts. "You know, there's more than one use for that powdered sugar."

He caressed her breasts everywhere except where she ached. Tender and swollen, she instinctively arched her back.

"So good," he muttered in approval. "You feel so good, Marley. Does it feel good to you?"

Her breath was tight in her chest. "Yes, but—"

"But what?" he asked, continuing to touch her breasts, but not her nipples. "Do you want more?"

The tension inside her growing, she managed a circular nod.

From the recesses of her mind, she saw him rub his fingers over the powdered pastry, then her nipples. "Oh my—" Her voice broke off. He looked deep in her eyes as he swirled his fingers around the turgid tips of her breasts. He was claiming her by inches. It was so erotic she almost couldn't bear to look.

Then, slowly, deliberately, he lowered his head and took her nipple into his mouth. His rough groan and her moan mingled together. He consumed her breast just as he'd taken her mouth, avidly, tenderly.

It wasn't enough for him to touch and take her. She wanted, needed, to touch and take him. She moved her hands in a searching caress down his chest.

Still sucking her breast, he stayed her hands with one of his.

Marley felt a sound of frustration bubble from her throat. "I need to touch you," she said, starting to tremble. "I need—"

Taking a breath, he drew back slightly to meet her gaze. His eyes were so dark and intense with desire that the power of his passion could have frightened her. But right now she wanted him too much. She wanted to know him, to learn him, to pleasure him.

Watching her all the while, he lowered her hand to his hard crotch. She caressed him, and he closed his eyes, lowering his zipper.

She took him, hot and full, in her hand and stroked him.

"I've dreamed of you touching me," he said. "I've dreamed of being inside you."

She felt the first drop of his honeyed desire, and an awesome need to pleasure and possess drove her on. She leaned closer to rub her open mouth against his.

Swearing, he shuddered and covered her hand with his. "We need to stop. I can't—"

"No," she said against his lips. "Let me. Please."

He swore again and wrapped his hand around the back of her neck. Drawing her mouth to his, he kissed her fully, sliding his tongue in and out of her mouth, filling her mind with erotic images.

Marley reveled in the power he gave her, caressing him until he jerked in pleasure, spilling himself into her palm as he groaned her name into her mouth.

"I'm gonna get you, Marley," Joe said, and it sounded like a vow.

* * *

"This is a mistake," Marley said, scowling at the stranger in the mirror. She took in the image of her artfully tousled hair, the subtle but seductive touch of makeup on her face, and the plunging neckline of the red dress she wore. She gave the dress a yank upward. "A big mistake."

"It is not." Her G.T.A. grabbed the hem and tugged the dress back in place. Lynn had insisted on *helping* Marley get ready for the formal banquet honoring Joe. "You obviously didn't play dress up enough as a child."

"Quit trying to analyze me," Marley grumbled. "This isn't *me*."

"Sure it is," Lynn said. "The dress fits perfectly. You can't wear jeans and those loose-fitting granny dresses everywhere."

"I know, but—"

"But nothing. You look gorgeous."

"I don't want to look gorgeous." The words popped out, surprising Marley as much as Lynn. She looked at Lynn. "Did I really just say that?"

Lynn nodded. "Yep."

"What I meant is that I've never wanted a man to be drawn to me strictly for how I look. And that hasn't been a problem."

"Of course not. The way you ugly down."

Marley blinked. "Ugly down?"

"It's like dummy down. You know, some women make themselves seem dumb to accommodate a man. What you do is a reverse kind of thing. You do nothing to accentuate how attractive you are, so you ugly down."

Marley felt a sinking sensation. Although Lynn's theory was convoluted, there was more than a grain of truth to it. She sighed and closed her eyes. "What I want is for a man to want me for who I am on the inside, but I'd also like him to appreciate what I look like."

She opened her eyes and winced at her reflection in the mirror. "And I don't want to be like the other women Joe has known in his life. I want to be different."

"Is he different from the other men you've known?"

Just thinking of Joe gave her a rush. "Oh, yes," she said, leading the way to the den.

Lynn must have read the emotions on Marley's face. "You've often had the upper hand in your other relationships, haven't you?"

Marley shrugged as she sat in an overstuffed chair across from Lynn. "I wouldn't have said so at the time. I would have said they were equal, give-and-take relationships."

"But?"

"But breaking off never devastated me. Even with my fiancé I was more bothered by the fact that I'd gotten out of balance with my work."

"With Joe it's different," Lynn ventured.

"Very."

"You don't have the upper hand."

"No."

Lynn grinned devilishly. "Fun, isn't it?"

Marley's lips twitched. "I wouldn't have chosen that word."

Lynn glanced at her watch and shot to her feet. "Oh my goodness, it's almost Super Stud time! I need to go." She looked at Marley. "You look gorgeous. Don't touch a thing."

"You don't need to rush. Joe's got a meeting, so he's sending a car. Remember? And what if my nose itches?" Marley mocked her.

"Twitch it. Honest, you look great even if it doesn't feel like you. Remember what you told me. Never give up a role you might need. And tonight you're—" She broke off, eyes narrowed in concentration.

"I'm not sure I want to hear this."

Lynn's face cleared. "You're Marley the Man-eater," she said as she raced out the door. "*Ciao*, babe."

"Man-eater," Marley echoed in consternation, then laughed and shook her head.

When the limo pulled in front of her house five minutes later, Marley shook her head again and considered bowing out. She felt out of her league. She immediately accused herself of being cowardly, so she grabbed a shawl and answered the doorbell.

The chauffeur offered her champagne, showed her the CD player and gave her instructions on how to operate the television. *Where's the Jacuzzi?* she almost asked.

When they pulled out of her neighborhood, she couldn't help but laugh. The last time she'd ridden in a limo, she'd been crammed in with ten of her high school buddies, one of whom had won the three-hour limo ride in a raffle.

Rain splattered against the windows, and Marley was glad she was safely in the limo. Trying to relax, she leaned back against the soft leather and closed her eyes as the chauffeur joined the rush hour traffic on the interstate.

Minutes later she felt the jarring impact of another vehicle smashing into the other side of the limo. Jolted, she clutched the cushion at the sound of metal crunching against metal.

The limo jerked to a stop, and the car behind them banged into the rear, pitching her forward. Her heart racing a mile a minute, she scrambled back into her seat. She felt another hard bounce, heard more crunching metal and whipped her head around to look behind her.

She winced as she braced herself for yet another collision. The row of cars lined up in rear-end collisions looked like an accordion. Except for the police cruiser zipping along the curb, traffic was at a standstill.

Hearing a tap at the window, she searched for the button and lowered it. "Miss, we've got an eight-car pileup," the officer said. "Since you're an eye witness, we need to take your statement. Please step into the patrol car."

Marley scrambled out of the limo into the rain. "But I'm expected downtown in less than half an hour."

"This won't take long."

Famous last words.

Seven

Stepping into the Tiffanylike glass-domed lobby of the Brown Palace Hotel, Marley searched in vain for a dry spot on her body. She was just shy of squishing when she walked. Certain her dress had shrunk two sizes, she wasn't looking forward to seeing her hair. It felt sticky and out of control.

She was determined, however, not to disappoint Joe. Since she'd encouraged him to attend the award dinner, the least she could do is join him as promised. Even if she looked like a Tasmanian she-devil. Aware of curious glances, she scanned the crowd and moved toward the powder room.

Halfway there, she heard her name.

"Marley!"

Her heart beat faster at the same time she cringed. She'd hoped to at least rearrange her hair before Joe set eyes on her. Shaking her head, she turned to him and smiled. "Guess what the wind blew in?"

Perfectly dressed in a black tux, he looked good enough to eat. He reminded her of a tiger temporarily restrained. Very temporarily. The classic black tux didn't conceal his muscular frame or the dangerous glint in his eyes that never quite went away.

He gave her a quick once-over and raised his eyebrows. "What happened?"

"Eight-car pileup," she told him, adjusting the neckline of her dress for the tenth time in as many minutes. "We were the second vehicle. Between making my statement in the police cruiser and running down a taxi, I had to do a few sprints in the rain."

Joe took her elbow and led her away from the crowd. "I'm glad you made it. I was beginning to wonder."

He watched her take a breath of relief. Her hair a mass of ringlets, her face flushed, she looked a little wild. Joe liked it. His gaze dropped to the shadow of her cleavage, and he couldn't help thinking it was a sin that she hid her curves behind long dresses and jeans and sweatshirts.

"That's some dress," he said, torn between tearing the clinging fabric from her and shielding her from other men's eyes by covering her with his jacket.

"Thanks. It looked better an hour ago," she said, completely missing his point. "I know I'm a mess, but if I could just have a couple of minutes—"

"Joe Caruthers!" a tall, statuesque blonde called

and pushed toward them. "You bad boy, I haven't seen you in ages. And you said you'd call," she said with a sexy pout.

Joe stifled a groan. "Kit, I've been busy." He felt Marley's curious gaze. "Marley Fuller, meet Kit—" He broke off, unable to recall her last name.

"Kit," Marley said in a friendly voice, extending her hand.

Impatience shimmered on Kit's exquisitely painted face. "Kit Carlton." She quickly shook Marley's hand, then turned back to Joe. "If you needed a date for tonight, you should have called me."

Joe wanted to haul Marley out of the hotel and forget the award. *What* had he seen in Kit? "Marley's my date," he said, gently urging Marley to the back of the room. "I'm sure a dozen guys were lined up for you."

Kit nearly purred. "I would have put you at the head of the line, Joe. My number's in the book," she called after them.

Joe made a strangled coughing sound.

"Kitty-cat got your tongue?" Marley asked with a smile that was a shade too sweet.

"Show some pity."

"Why? She's beautiful. Her hair is fixed. She's dry."

"She's a pain. The reason her eyes are green is because she has dollar signs flashing in them."

"Sounds a little jaded, cynical—"

"And true," he said, then pulled her closer. "Let's forget this and go to my place."

Marley shook her head, but he could see that she

was tempted. "No. We're here so you can accept your award."

He dipped his head to brush his mouth against her ear and was gratified with the quick breath she took. "I don't care about the award," he told her. "If they want to thank me for being a nice guy, they can thank me with—"

"Dead presidents. I know." She leaned into him for a half second, then pulled back. "This is beginning to feel like a quest for me. Plus, I'm starting to get hungry."

"I will get you *anything* you want to eat if we leave now. Hell, I'll fly in champagne from Paris if—"

Marley shook her head. "Just give me a minute. I need to fix my hair."

"Don't touch it," Joe said.

She paused, blinking.

"Don't," he repeated. "I like it."

She met his gaze dead-on. "When was your last eye examination?"

Joe's lips twitched. "I've got twenty-twenty vision. The only change I would make is to ditch the dress."

"You and me both," she muttered, tugging at the neck as she turned away. "I was out of my mind to buy this."

Unable to let that pass, he snagged her wrist, stopping her mid-step. "Marley," he said.

He heard her take another careful quick breath.

"I'm gonna get you," he told her.

She shivered, then surprised him by whirling

around. Her eyes met his in a sensual challenge he'd never seen from her before. Boldly feminine, she might as well have put her hand on his crotch. He was hard just from her expression.

She cocked her head to one side. "We'll see."

Joe narrowed his eyes as he watched her flounce off. The urge to possess her throbbed in every pulse point of his body. She had no idea how close he came to following her into the powder room, throwing her over his shoulder and letting her *see* how much he wanted her.

Marley caught sight of her hair in the mirror and swallowed a sound of distress. It was almost enough to make her swear, and Marley had given up swearing years ago when she'd learned that kids walked into conversations at the most inconvenient moments.

A tall, brunette woman made a tsking sound as she meticulously applied lipstick. "Bad time to get caught in a rainstorm, isn't it?"

"Yes," Marley said, glumly adjusting the neck of her dress again. She grabbed a paper towel and blotted her shiny face.

"Was that Joe Caruthers I saw you with?" the brunette continued.

Marley sighed and nodded. "Yes. He's getting a service award tonight."

"I know." The woman smiled and capped her lipstick. "I used to date him."

Two in one night? Marley quickly scanned the bathroom, wondering who else...

"He's an exceptional man," the woman said.

Her heart squeezed tight. "Yes, he is."

"And exceptionally fast about moving on, once he's lost interest." She met Marley's gaze. "Good luck."

After that, Marley let her hair down, literally. Joe would eventually move on and leave her. Did she want him even if it was just for a while? The question tore at her, but she couldn't escape the answer.

Yes, she did, she thought, watching Joe's veiled impatience as the speaker repeated his various acts of charity and generosity. She wanted him.

Putting her hand on his arm, she caught his eye and smiled. What was the saying? "If you're going to walk on thin ice, you may as well dance." Her sense of fate about Joe was stronger than ever. Her heart couldn't stop racing, as if she were flying down a ski slope. Marley had never been a good skier.

She mentally switched gears. "Would it be easier if he were insulting you?" she whispered, nodding toward the presenter.

He threaded his fingers through her hair. "It's hell on my digestion. Let's go."

Marley muffled her laughter. "Just a little longer."

He gave a quick tug of her hair. "You've turned into a tease."

She shook her head. "Not me."

"You know what a tease is, don't you?" he asked in a low voice.

Marley's heartbeat picked up again. "Of course I do."

"A tease is someone who promises," Joe told her.

Marley nodded. "But doesn't deliver."

His dark gaze, full of heart-stopping, thigh-melting questions, met hers.

Her throat felt tight and achy at the path she was taking, but Marley was decided. She swallowed. "I deliver," she said softly.

She knew immediately by the conviction on his face that her fate was sealed.

Joe glanced at his speedometer and deliberately backed off the accelerator, even though his instinct was to floor it. Marley attempted to make conversation, and he gave monosyllabic responses.

He needed to possess her.

It was ridiculous how much he wanted her. He'd told himself that too many times to count over the past weeks. He wanted to lose himself in the scent, taste and feel of her. He wanted every possible intimacy with this woman, and whatever he got from her just made him want more. Hiding the intensity of his passion for her had become impossible.

"Joe, why are you so quiet?" She curled her hand around his arm and leaned toward him, her breast rubbing against his arm.

Withholding a moan, he chuckled wryly to himself. "Because I'm trying to get you home before I rip that dress off you and ravage you."

Silence followed, but she didn't pull away. He glanced at her, wondering what her thoughts were. "Did I scare you?"

"You always scare me," Marley said.

Joe took the interstate exit for his house. "Then

why haven't you padlocked your door and given me my walking papers?''

"Because I'm not sure what I'm more scared of. Your feelings for me or—'' she took a careful breath "—my feelings for you.''

She spoke from the heart, and Joe felt the tenderness trickle into his passion for her. A surprising feeling, but it didn't dilute his need for her. It was too great and had been denied too long. "I've never wanted a woman like I want you.''

He glanced at her once more and saw her eyes dip close.

"Show me,'' she said softly.

He took her hand and pressed it against his aching arousal. She paused, then caressed him.

Swearing, he began to play blackjack in his mind to keep him sane until he got her home. Barely giving the garage door time to open, he pulled in and jerked to a stop. Then he unfastened his seat belt and hers, pulled her into his arms and took her mouth the way he planned to take her body. Thoroughly.

Her mouth joined his, her tongue tangling sweetly with his. He sucked in a shallow breath and smelled her scent, the fragrance of her feminine arousal. It teased him mercilessly.

He devoured her lips, sucking her bottom lip, tasting her until she clung to him. Touching her bare shoulders beneath her dress, he wanted to put his hands all over her. He tried to push the dress down, but was only partly successful.

Rolling her nipples in his fingers, he groaned with need. "Dammit, this dress—''

"I know," Marley murmured, pressing her breasts against his palms in a way that made him shudder. "I told the clerk it was wrong for me."

Her sentence barely permeating his brain, he gave a rough laugh. "That's not what I meant," he said. "It's just too damn hard to get off."

Marley pulled back, her eyes hazy with passion, her lips already swollen from his kisses. "Oh."

The sight of her willing and waiting was too much. Joe swore again. He wanted full and complete access. "I'll buy you another," he told her, then took the red fabric in his hands and ripped it straight down.

Marley's eyes widened in surprise.

"I'll buy you two more, three more," he said, and carried her out his car door and into his house.

"What are you doing?" she asked, appearing to have difficulty forming the words.

Joe strode up the stairs to his bedroom. "I'm *showing* you."

And show her, he did.

Marley kept wondering when she would catch her breath, but he took it and kept it.

Spilling her onto his big bed, he followed her down and dropped his head to her breasts, nuzzling her as he pushed down her stockings. His dark head on her light skin was an erotic sight she almost couldn't bear to watch.

"I'm moving too fast," he muttered. "Too fast, but it's been too long."

His hands searched between her legs and found her wet and wanting. He made her femininity buzz and her blood roar. She pushed ineffectually at his shirt. "Joe. I want—I need—"

He stripped off his shirt, baring his muscular chest. "Oh, Marley, you're so wet, so sweet," he told her, moving his mouth down her belly to her thighs.

"Oh, my—" Marley's voice stopped when his lips found her and then his tongue. He wove a shameless magic over her, rendering her completely vulnerable, yet launched her into a whole new galaxy of pleasure.

The tension was so sharp and sweet she was clawing at the bedspread. The first wave hit, and she stiffened, crying out, riding crest after crest, the pleasure taking her in bursts. With trembling hands, she urged him upward.

"I need you," she whispered, her voice husky. "I need you," she told him, staring into his dark, dark eyes, "in me."

"Oh, Marley," he said, kissing her.

Determination, need, love drove her. She pushed down his trousers and briefs and found him hard.

"Sweetheart, don't do that," he told her. "I can't—" His growl rumbled through her inside and out. "I'm on a short string—"

"Doesn't feel short to me," she murmured, still stroking him.

Giving a sound between a groan and a laugh, he pulled a plastic packet from his slacks and pushed his clothes all the way off. "No more teasing," he said, quickly putting on the condom.

"Now, you're—" with one sure stroke, he thrust inside her and shuddered "—mine. All mine."

With his gaze locked on hers, he moved in a mind-robbing rhythm until he soared over the edge with his jagged, hot release. And Marley had never been so completely and irrevocably *taken*.

They made love again and again during the night. It seemed they barely rested before he was reaching for her or she was curling against him.

When dawn filtered though the curtains in Joe's room, Marley awoke, feeling as if she'd run a marathon. Her body felt tender, her muscles sore. She looked at Joe sleeping beside her and was overcome with wonder. His dark hair was tousled over his closed eyelids, his naked body a study in strength. He reminded her of a conqueror.

What did that make her? she wondered, and decided to get a drink of water. Easing toward the side of the bed, she was stopped by his arm around her waist. He pulled her back.

"Where do you think you're going?"

Her heart hammered as she met his gaze. "I'm thirsty. I was going to get some water."

"Stay here," he said, rising from the bed. "I'll get it."

"I don't mind," she stammered. "I can—" She stopped when he disappeared into the master bath.

He immediately returned with a glass of water and arranged her against his chest as she drank it all. Toying with her hair, he kissed her cheek. His tenderness plucked at her heart.

"More?" he asked.

She shook her head, surprised she didn't feel at all

self-conscious of her nudity. She couldn't remember feeling this at ease.

He lifted a finger to her forehead. "What's going on in here?"

She closed her eyes. "I'm a little wobbly all over."

"But you're thinking?"

"I'm *trying* to," she said, and laughed to herself. "My brain feels like a bunch of loose marbles rolling around."

"Then you need to stay in bed," he said, and before she knew it his warm mouth was on her nipple.

Marley's eyes popped open. She *couldn't* want him again, but she felt her inside grow soft and fluid. "You can't want me again," she managed.

"Yes, I can, and I do," he told her, pulling her closer, his erection rubbing against her thigh. "It's Sunday, and I'm going to keep you in my bed all day long."

He nibbled at the tips of her breasts, making her deliciously restless. "What about food?" she asked with the fraction of her mind that was still operating.

"Delivery. Whatever you want," he said, running his hand over and between her thighs. "Hell, I can have lobster flown in from Maine."

She gasped when he slid his finger inside her. "I don't want lobster." Disconcerted by his ability to render her boneless, she pushed him slightly away. "A bowl of cereal or a bagel would be nice," she said, and took her turn kissing her way down his abdomen.

Her mouth hovered inches from his hardness, and he groaned. "A bagel. You want a bagel?"

Hearing the desperation in his voice, she smiled. "Later." Then she lowered her mouth to him.

The next few weeks were a blur of discovery and joy for Marley. She suspected Joe felt the same way because he spent every possible minute with her.

He always wanted her to stay at his house, and it had become a running joke what his next reason or excuse would be. The latest, "What if my pipes freeze?" didn't fly with Marley. It was mid-August, and she won this match primarily because Joe was scheduled to go out of town.

It amazed her and stole her heart that he wanted her at his home even when he wouldn't be there. This time, however, she needed to get a very important question answered.

She had fallen so totally in love with Joe that she wasn't sure which answer she hoped for from the at-home pregnancy test. The morning would tell.

Eight

"**H**ow's the sleepyhead?" Joe asked Marley and offered her a cup of coffee. They enjoyed his rooftop balcony so much, they'd made a habit of eating a light breakfast there in the mornings.

Marley quelled the urge to wrinkle her nose. She usually loved both the taste and smell of coffee, but lately, nothing tasted good to her. She lifted her hand and shook her head. "No, thanks…this time. I think I might get some juice in a little bit."

He studied her. "You okay?"

She smiled and hugged him, wondering if now was the time she should tell him. She'd been looking for the best possible moment. "I'm fine. Just not hungry."

"You've seemed tired lately. Maybe you can sleep a little extra during the break before fall semester."

Marley nodded, spotting a school bus in the valley. "True. You've worn me out."

He gave her a gentle pinch. "Works both ways."

She kissed his cheek and squeezed him again, then pointed at the bus. "Public school starting already."

He took a drink of his coffee and nodded. "Yep. The boys at camp finished the tree house and signed their names to it for posterity. You had a good idea."

"For a shrink," she said with a quick smile.

He cracked a grin. "Yeah."

Her heart hammering against her rib cage, she kept her voice calm. "You ever thought about having children?"

He stiffened. "Yep. I thought about it."

She held her breath. "And?"

"And I decided it would be a terrible idea."

Marley's heart sank to her feet. "Why?"

"Tin man, remember?" he said with a wry smile, knocking at his chest. "No heart. I'd make a rotten father."

Everything inside her protested. "That's not true. You're a very compassionate man. Not only that, you show your compassion in practical ways."

He shook his head and smiled. "That's what you keep trying to tell me."

"The only thing I'm doing is holding up a mirror so you can see yourself more clearly."

"You might hold the mirror, but I hold the crystal ball, and fatherhood is *not* in my future." He dropped a kiss on her forehead. "You don't have anything to worry about, Marley. I'm as careful as a man can be."

* * *

Five days later Joe listened to Marley's voice message on his answering machine for the tenth time.

"Hi, Joe. I've decided to take advantage of my break with a spur-of-the-moment trip. I know you're busy with your new store opening, so you shouldn't miss me too much. Take care of yourself. I'll talk to you when I get back."

Frowning, he paced the floor of his den and played the message once more. Her voice sounded different—tight and a little husky. She spoke in a rush, as if she was running away. The notion bothered the hell out of him.

What bothered him more was how much he'd missed her. He'd grown accustomed to waking with her in his arms. He'd gotten used to seeing the laughter shining in her eyes. Her voice wrapped around him like moonlight, and her body fit his like a glove.

Although his craving for her hadn't diminished, he'd relaxed with it, because she'd made it okay with her love for him. Joe didn't fool himself. He knew Marley loved him. If any other woman had revealed that emotion to him, she would have been out the door. If any other woman had expressed her love for him, he would have suspected her motives.

But not Marley. He trusted her; perhaps more than he should. Where was she? Why had she left so abruptly? He'd *missed* her. Too much. The unease in his gut grew. The clock on the mantel chimed ten o'clock. If she arrived home late, she might not call because she wouldn't want to *bother* him.

Joe gave a rough chuckle and headed for his Sub-

urban. He figured he couldn't get much more bothered than he was now. When he saw her car in her
driveway, the relief that swept over him was embar-
rassing. He parked his car and knocked on her front
door.

She answered, wearing a robe and nightgown.

"How's the world traveler?" he asked, grinning
at the dismay on her face.

She shook her head and glanced away as she let
him in. "Not the world, just Cheyenne."

"Cheyenne? Why'd you go there?"

"I heard it was quiet."

"Unless you go during Frontier Days, I guess it
is," Joe said, and pulled her into his arms, relishing
her soft, clean scent. "I missed you," he confessed.
"You should have told me you wanted to get away.
I would have gone with you."

"You were busy. I slept a lot. You would have
been bored."

He heard the tightness in her voice again and
pulled back slightly to look at her again. There were
faint circles under her eyes, and her skin was more
pale than usual. He frowned. "Are you sick?"

Marley sighed, turning away from him. She
wrapped her arms around herself as if she needed a
hug and walked toward the den. "Not right now."

Concern raced through him. Joe shot to her side.
"What does that mean?"

"It means I need to talk to you, but I was hoping
to wait until tomorrow morning."

Joe's gut clenched. He didn't like the sound of
this. "I think you'd better start talking now."

Marley sank into a chair and covered her face with one hand. "Okay. You need to sit down."

"Why?"

"Just sit down," she said in the most impatient voice he'd ever heard her use.

Joe took a deep breath and sat down.

She rubbed her forehead. "There's no easy way to tell you this."

"Marley," he said, his own impatience coating his voice.

"I'm pregnant."

Her words hit him like a blow to the head. He was unable to speak for a full moment. He blinked like a stunned rodeo rider. "No."

"Yes." She leaned her head back and stared at the ceiling.

"It's not possible."

"Yes, it is."

"We used protection."

"I know. One time it apparently didn't work."

Everything inside Joe rejected the possibility. He fought a deluge of ugly memories. Unable to sit, he began to pace the length of the room. "I know I used protection every time. *Every time*," he emphasized. "I'm very careful."

"I know."

He heard the weariness in her tone, but his mind and stomach were churning. He turned to face her and met her gaze dead-on. "Are you sure it was me?"

Her eyes widened with hurt, and she gave a soft

humorless laugh. "It was either you or immaculate conception."

"I need you to tell me the truth. It couldn't have been me," he insisted.

"It couldn't have been anyone *but* you. However, if you need a blood test—"

Joe swore viciously. Why had this happened? Why had she let this happen? Part of him protested his accusation of her, but he was too angry, too hurt. This was too close to what had happened before.

"You asked me about having children," he said in the calmest voice he could manage.

Her face pinched with tension, she nodded. "I—" she breathed deeply "—I already knew and wanted to find out how you would feel about it."

"I don't want children."

"It's too late."

"No, it's not."

Her gaze turned cool. "Yes," she said with rock-solid certainty. "It is."

Joe was full of every negative emotion he could imagine: hurt, disillusionment, loss. He narrowed his eyes. He'd been fooled again. "Another woman told me she was pregnant with my baby. She tried to trick me into marrying her, but she didn't get away with it. You won't, either," he told her. "I won't ask you to marry me."

"Good," she said with an awesome strength, considering her weariness. "Because my answer would be no."

In the silence that followed, Joe would have sworn

he heard a shredding sound. It took him a full moment to realize the shredding was inside him.

Marley stood, and her remote expression tore at him even more.

"I'm tired. I want you to leave now."

Joe stared at her, angry at himself, her and everyone. *Why had this happened?* Everything had been so good. Now it was all gone.

As soon as the door closed behind Joe, Marley collapsed into the chair and drew her knees up to her chest. She'd never felt such loss. Her chest and throat were tight, and her heart hurt.

She should have been more careful. She shouldn't have allowed the pregnancy to happen, she told herself for the hundredth time. Yet she knew they'd taken precautions every time.

Her eyes began to burn, and she buried her head in her hands. She felt so lonely, so alone.

The image of his accusing face echoed through her mind. Her heart twisted. Knowing that Joe didn't want children, she should have predicted his reaction. After spending the past several days in Cheyenne rehearsing what she would say to Joe and imagining a variety of responses, she should have been prepared for his anger.

A tiny, crazy part of her, however, had hoped things would be different. Some resilient kernel inside her had wished that Joe could fall in love with her the way she had fallen in love with him. Even though Marley had painted a dark picture to prepare herself, when she'd gone to sleep, she'd dreamed Joe had adjusted and they'd been happy together with their baby.

A powerful blow of grief shook her. Joe had brought her magic in a way she'd never known. Giving him up hurt. Oh, how it hurt. Her pent-up emotions burst free, and she began to sob.

"Oh, Joe," she whispered through her tears. "Did it have to go so wrong?"

Joe didn't fall asleep until the wee hours of the morning, and before he was fully awake, he slid his fingers over the covers in search of Marley. Empty-handed, he opened his eyes and felt her absence in his gut. His body kicked in first, then his mind, with the signs of withdrawal.

She was gone and wouldn't be back. Bittersweet memories flooded his mind. It was all too easy to remember her touch, her smile and the way she'd focused her undivided attention on him. All too easy to remember her scent and the way she'd felt when he'd buried himself inside her. And it was easy to remember he'd been a fool to believe she was different from the other women he'd known.

He didn't want her back, he told himself ruthlessly.

Throwing off the covers, he squinted his eyes at the sun shining brightly through his bedroom window and rose from his bed. He might feel gray inside, but it was just another sunny day in Colorado.

Life would go on, he assured himself as he strode into the shower and turned the water on full force. It might take a little longer than usual, but he would forget Marley Fuller.

But what about the baby? a small voice inside him asked.

Joe's heart twisted in another knot. It was early days. He would settle that score later. Right now he had to concentrate on how much he did not want Marley, and the best way to accomplish that was by plunging himself into his business.

Over the next week Joe worked twelve- and fourteen-hour days. Each night, however, he dreamed of Marley. Laughing or serious, she'd always reminded him of the good inside him. In his dreams she soothed and aroused him, loving him with her heart, mind and body. Every morning he awoke aroused, eager to see her smile and hear her voice. Every morning he reached for her.

Catching sight of the involuntary way his fingers clenched the sheet, he swore and pushed out of bed. He stomped into the bathroom and looked into the mirror. Funny how he'd avoided looking at himself during the past week.

He saw mussed hair and a jaw in need of a shave, hollow eyes with circles underneath and cynicism in every line and groove.

What about the baby?

What if you were wrong about her?

The small voice he'd drowned out with work, radio and TV, got louder. Sighing, he squeezed the bridge of his nose and listened and thought.

The prickly uneasiness that had plagued him during the past week nagged at him again. Marley's behavior was totally different from that of the woman who had deceived him years ago. Marley hadn't called him. She hadn't asked for marriage or money. She hadn't asked for anything.

His chest tightened. What if the contraception had failed and she *was* carrying his baby? What if she was caught off guard by the pregnancy as much as he was?

Could he abandon his child? The mere thought made him feel like throwing up. After what his father had done, Joe would never abandon his child. No matter what the cost.

Sitting in her office, Marley sipped the herbal tea that promised to provide peace and tranquility. She prayed it would help keep her breakfast down. Over the past few days, she had alternated between numbness and breathtaking pain. In the hovel she'd created of her life, though, she found a purpose in her baby. It wasn't a purpose she'd planned, but she was determined to do her best.

She checked her watch, thankful her office hours were nearly over. Since it was the beginning of the semester, most students weren't behind enough to be pounding on her door for help.

She heard a tap at her door and gave a wry laugh. She'd counted her blessings too soon. "Come in," she called, and in walked Joe.

Marley nearly choked on her tea. She coughed, swallowed and dropped her mug on her desk. Gaping at him, she mopped up the drops that had sloshed over the rim.

"What a surprise," she managed to say.

Joe closed the door behind him and remained standing, with his hands in his pockets. "I wondered how you were doing," he said.

Feeling his intense scrutiny, she resisted the urge to straighten her hair. "The phone's great for that, but I'm fine. And you?"

"Okay," he said. "Busy with the new franchise."

Their stilted conversation was like another stab from a thorn. Their communication had once been so free and easy. Torn between asking him to sit down or leave, to calm her nerves, she did neither. "It must be going well."

"Yeah." He ran his hand through his hair, and the gesture drew her attention to his muscular frame. Her heart caught as her body remembered being held by him, making love with him.

"Have you seen a doctor?"

Marley swallowed. "Yes. Everything looks fine, and I'm taking the vitamins."

"I missed you."

I missed you, too. She didn't say it, couldn't say it. It had taken her the past month to come to grips with the fact that a lasting love relationship with Joe wasn't in the cards.

She lifted her shoulders. "I don't know what to say. You made your feelings fairly clear."

"As mud," Joe murmured. "Your getting pregnant caught me off guard. After my head cleared, I wondered if maybe you were telling the truth. Maybe you *weren't* trying to trap me."

Marley's blood burned at the insinuation. She'd

worked through enough of the pain to find anger. "I did tell you the truth," she told him, "and you can be sure I wasn't trying to trap you."

Giving in to her frustration, she stood. "Listen, Joe, I don't want you to ask me to marry you. I don't expect your support. I certainly don't want *any* of your money." She took a breath and met his gaze with a strength born of nights spent in quiet desperation. "I can handle this. I can have this baby and love and raise him or her. And I don't need you to do any of it."

He raised his eyebrows in surprise. "What if I'm the father?"

Marley ground her teeth, feeling her temper heat. "You *are* the father, but since you said you don't want children, you can consider your contribution finished."

His eyes narrowed, and he moved toward her. "And if I've changed my mind? If I've decided I'm going to take care of my responsibilities?" he asked in a low, determined tone that shook her.

Surprised, she sat down and grappled with her confusion. "I...I...don't know. You told me you didn't want children," she said, unable to keep the accusation from her voice.

"You took me by surprise. I needed time to adjust."

If he changed his mind about wanting a child, could he change his mind about his feelings for her? Marley slammed the door on that possibility. She refused to consider it. If she couldn't count on him to trust her, then she couldn't count on him for love.

"Are you saying you *want* this child?"

He took a careful breath and plowed his fingers through his hair again. "I'll be honest. I'm not there, yet. But I would never let my child grow up without a father."

Marley was struck by the turbulence and pride in his dark eyes. Even though she knew there was no future for them, she could still feel his turmoil as if it were her own. "This sounds like an obligation."

"This is a man's responsibility," he said without an ounce of give in his voice or on his face.

If he carried through with his intentions, she would be connected to Joe for the rest of her life through their child. Marley didn't know if she could bear it. She shook her head. "I don't know what to say. I thought you were out of the picture. I'm going to have to think about this."

He leaned over her desk and met her gaze. "You can think about it all you want, but you're carrying my baby. and my baby *will* know his father."

Marley's stomach flipped at the resolute glint in his eyes.

"Here's something else you should think about. I believe my child should have my name. I think the mother of my child should have my name."

Panic raced through her. Marley automatically shook her head and held up her hand. "Oh, no. I can't stop you from being involved with your child. It would be morally wrong. I couldn't do it. But this is not the Dark Ages. I don't need to marry you so you can slap your name on me and the baby."

"I want this child to be legitimate."

"I'm won't marry you for some outdated over-rated sense of legitimacy. Single mothers make up a significant percentage of the population."

"I had a single mother. I know what it's like. I know what the child doesn't get."

Marley bit her tongue. He was remembering his experience, and he had strong feelings about it. She couldn't blame him for that. Neither could she buckle under to his pressure. "I'm different from your mother," she said gently. "I'm sure she did the best she could, but my education is different. My socio-economic status is different."

She felt a stab of pain as she remembered how Joe had accused her of trying to trap him last week. She smiled sadly. "You obviously didn't know me well enough, because I'm also different from that woman who lied because she wanted you to marry her. But I guess it's too late for that."

Nine

Eyes closed, Marley stuck her face in front of the fan and pictured herself on a cool, northeastern beach looking at the ocean with the wind blowing in her face. The image soothed her nerves and helped calm the nausea that had plagued her during the past two weeks.

Her doorbell rang.

Marley groaned and walked carefully to her front door. She rolled her eyes, recalling Lynn's crack about how Marley had started to walk like a shipboard drunk. She opened the door to Joe. Her heart jumped, and she scolded herself for the immediate response.

He stared at her and frowned. "You're pale. You look awful."

Just what she wanted to hear. "Thank you for

sharing that. I'll be happy to talk with you later, but right now I'm doing my antinausea therapy.'' She tried to close the door, but he planted his foot in the way.

He quirked an eyebrow. ''Antinausea therapy?''

In no mood to fight a man who seemed to have a will as strong as God, she turned away from him. ''The fan,'' she said, when she sank down in front of the box fan again. ''I'm on a northeastern beach in the winter. The water is beautiful, and the breeze has enough bite to make my lungs feel clean.''

''You can't take anything for it?''

Hearing his voice close to her, she had difficulty holding the image of the beach. Instead, she smelled his clean, masculine scent, felt his warmth, and thought of how his arms felt around her. She remembered the power of his passion and his body when he made love to her. Despite the fan, her cheeks heated.

''I can't take anything for the nausea. If this doesn't work, I'm thinking about some kind of witch doctor's dance.''

She felt him lift her hair off the back of her neck. ''How many times have you been sick?''

''Every morning for the past two weeks. I was enjoying the fact that I could be sick all by myself since it was Sunday,'' she said, trying to keep the grumble from her voice.

''Until I showed up,'' he said with a chuckle.

She felt the whisper of his breath cooling the back of her neck when he laughed. An intimate image of her naked body tangled with his obliterated the ocean picture. Marley bit her lip and opened her eyes.

"You're too pale. Are you sure you're okay?" Joe asked in a low voice that made her heart catch.

"The doctor says the baby is fine. In fact, some studies indicate that first-trimester nausea is a good sign. It means my hormones are kicking in the way they're supposed to."

Except for the whir of the fan, silence followed. Marley glanced away from the fan to Joe.

He chuckled and met her gaze.

"What?" she asked.

He sifted his fingers through her hair and shot her a wry look. "The first time I saw you, you made my hormones kick in *more* than they're supposed to."

Marley took a careful breath. She was trapped by his hand in her hair and more profoundly by his gaze. There was heat and a flicker of tenderness in his dark eyes. The tenderness could have undid her, untied her like shoestrings on a sneaker.

He wove his other hand through one of hers, meshing his callused skin against hers. His fingers tangled with hers, the way their lives had become.

Joe's accusations still rang in her ears, though, and Marley pulled her hand from his. She instinctively wrapped her arms around herself. She couldn't open herself that way to him again. If she had relied on her better judgment instead of her instincts and emotions, then her life would be very different now. *But would her life have been better?* her conscience prodded.

She shook her hair from his fingers and stood. "I'll feel better soon."

Joe joined her. "Can I get you some breakfast?"

Marley wrinkled her nose. "No, thanks. I don't like the way breakfast food smells."

"Coffee?"

She grimaced. "I don't like the way much of anything smells."

"You have to eat," Joe insisted.

"I do," she said walking toward the kitchen. "I eat soda crackers and graham crackers and prenatal vitamins. In fact, I'm going to eat some right now."

"I want to go with you to your doctor."

Marley blinked and looked at him. "Why?"

His jaw tightened. "I want to meet your doctor. He should know—"

"She," Marley corrected.

Joe nodded briskly. "She should know the father."

Marley felt a rush of conflicting feelings, but tried to be reasonable. "Okay. You can go sometime. Maybe for the ultrasound?"

He nodded. "Yeah, but I'll go next time, too."

Reluctant for Joe to invade her life again, she frowned as she pulled down the box of crackers. "The visits are boring."

"I'll still go," he said, his tone firm.

"Joe, they don't do anything very amazing. Weigh me, measure my uterus, take a urine sample, check my blood pressure, listen for the baby's heartbeat—"

His eyes widened in surprise. "Already? You've listened to the baby's heartbeat already?"

The wonder on his face tugged at her, but she felt pulled in two opposing directions. Marley had known and loved Joe too well to not let him know and love their baby. Every minute she was with Joe, however, cut like a razor. She wondered if she could bear it.

He caught her humming in front of the small fan he'd sent her at work. Though her blond hair was pulled back in a white ribbon, it was flying in the fan's breeze, and her vibrating hum made her sound like a little kid.

Despite the fact that she'd changed his life in ways he'd planned to avoid, he was still drawn to her. She was an odd woman, full of color and emotion. There was so much he still didn't know about her. So much he would never know, he realized, because their relationship was irrevocably changed. Watching her made him feel his aloneness.

Shaking off the feeling, he knocked on the inside of the doorjamb. "Gone to the beach again?"

She whipped around with an expression of chagrin and laughter. "No. My mom called earlier today, and I had a little attack of nostalgia. I remember sitting in front of the fan in the kitchen with my brother singing songs like 'Row, Row, Row Your Boat.' Thank you for the fan. It was thoughtful."

He nodded, remembering a fan in his mother's apartment. With no siblings and his mother working two jobs, he'd often been left alone. "Does your mother know you're pregnant?"

Marley's smile fell. "Not yet. I thought I'd wait a couple more weeks. I haven't made all my plans yet.

You should never be your own shrink, but I'm thinking about things like having a support system and the fact that this job was originally intended as a temporary offer."

Joe's heart stopped. "You're not leaving."

She looked away. "I haven't made any firm decisions. I'm just doing a lot of thinking. The college wants me to stay, which means I'll get health benefits, but—"

Alarmed and impatient, Joe cut to the chase. "If we got married, it would solve all these problems."

Silent for a full moment Marley met his gaze. "And create others," she pointed out quietly. "There are other things to consider, like when I have to go back to work after the baby's born and having someone to call for emergencies."

"You'll call *me* for emergencies," he said emphatically. "And I'll hire a mother's helper for the baby."

Marley looked at the ceiling as if she were searching for help. "Thank you. But you can't buy someone who's going to tell me what to do about colic in the middle of the night or someone who will reassure me that everything really will turn out all right."

She met his gaze with eyes that searched deeper than the trappings of his success, deeper than his skin. He felt it all the way to his tin heart.

An hour later he watched a nurse weigh Marley, check her blood pressure, then he joined her in the examination room.

A middle-aged woman whisked into the room with a brisk smile. "Good afternoon, Dr. Fuller. Everything's looking good. I'm Dr. Smithson,'' she said, extending her hand to Joe.

"I'm Joe Caruthers. I'm—'' he hesitated "—the father.'' In that moment his fate was sealed. He wouldn't need a blood test for proof. He knew the truth deep in his bones.

"Hi, Dad,'' Dr. Smithson said as she moved toward Marley. "Would you like to hear your baby's ticker?''

"Yes.''

After a brief examination the doctor put her stethoscope on Marley's abdomen. A second passed and Joe heard a rapid swishing sound.

His gaze met Marley's, and he knew the wonder on her face was mirrored on his.

"It's fast, isn't it?'' she whispered.

Nodding, he reached for Marley's hand. His chest tightened. This woman would give him a baby. She would make him a father, a role he'd thought he never wanted. But now everything was different. He wanted the child.

He looked at Marley's smile and felt the tingling sensation in his hand. She squeezed his hand. Unable to look away from her, he just stared. He was on a tidal wave of emotion and an earthshaking realization. Yes, he wanted the child.

He also wanted the woman.

"I want you to think about getting a different car,'' Joe told her as he invaded her house yet again on Saturday morning.

Marley looked at him quizzically as he handed her

a croissant dusted with powdered sugar and herbal tea. "Thank you. I might be able to eat this," she murmured, and took a bite.

"About your car," Joe continued.

"My car's fine. It shouldn't snow for another month or so, right?"

Joe tossed her a pitying glance. "It could snow tomorrow. I think you need something larger."

Marley took another bite of the croissant.

"I'll buy it," he told her.

"That's not necessary," she quickly said.

"Think of it as an investment in safety for the baby."

She frowned, taking a sip of tea. "I don't want your money."

Joe sighed. He'd never heard those words from a woman's mouth, and he'd never thought those words would irritate the hell out of him. "You need to get over that. I'm not suffering, and I don't want you or our child to suffer."

"I'm not suffering," she said, but it felt like a lie. She still missed Joe. Every night and every morning.

"We could just go look," he told her. "Looking can't hurt."

"That's a matter of opinion," she muttered, thinking of how looking at Joe still hurt. She took another bite and washed it down with a sip of tea.

"We need to cooperate," he said, moving closer. "We're going to be parents of the same child."

Marley sighed. He was right, but...

Joe leaned still closer and rubbed his index finger over her lips.

She stood stock-still, holding her breath as she watched him lick his finger. It was such an intimate gesture she had to swallow hard over the lump in her throat. "Why did you do that?"

"You had sugar on your mouth." His gaze dipped to her lips, and Marley felt the familiar, powerful, but terrible, pull toward him. His mouth lifted in a half grin. "I just thought I'd help."

After checking three car lots, Marley never wanted to buy another car in her life.

"The Buick was perfect," Joe told her.

"It was a tank," Marley said as she sank into the seat of his Suburban.

"You said that about all of them," he muttered.

"All of the ones *you* liked. I like having a smaller car. It's easier to get in and out of parking spaces without bumping into other cars."

"What about the Cadillac?"

"We already have one," she said on impulse, immediately horrified she'd said *we*. Rattled, she quickly corrected herself. "*You* already have one. Don't you remember the sales guy said the nickname for a Suburban is a Colorado Cadillac?" She glanced at his hard profile. "Besides, I have no interest in spending that much money on a car."

"I would buy it," he said.

Marley rolled her eyes. "I don't want you to buy it."

"Why?"

"Because I'm not your responsibility," she told

him, and she heard pride, her father's pride, creeping into her voice.

He stopped at a stoplight and looked at her. "Is that what you think? That you're not my responsibility?"

Renewed anger and unhealed hurt trickled over old wounds like salt water. "I know I'm not your responsibility," she said heatedly. "The very idea of being a responsibility or 'obligation,'" she said, hating the word, "makes me feel like throwing up. I don't want a penny from you. I never did. Your money wasn't what I was interested in."

Tears sprang to her eyes, and she searched for the button for the electric windows. "Why isn't this—"

"I keep them locked," he said, and looked away to release them.

Marley felt as if she were going to burst. When they stopped at a light she noticed they were in the right-hand lane. She double-checked for safety, then moved purely on instinct. Too emotional to remain with him one more minute, she pushed open the car door and released her seat belt. "I'm sorry, but I can't stay. I—"

"What the hell?"

Joe reached for her, but she scooted out the door before he could catch her. Past the roar of confusion in her head, she heard Joe yelling for her and the beep of a car horn. She quickly skipped to the side of the road and ran toward the strip mall close by.

Spotting a department store behind the row of shops, Marley headed for that. Her heart was pounding, she was perspiring and crying, and all she wanted was to get lost in the crowd for a few moments.

She wiped the tears from her cheeks with the back of her hands and walked through the automatic doors. The store hummed with activity, and Marley walked aimlessly through the aisles trying to work through her confusion.

It wasn't like her to act so impulsively, but she'd been doing more of that since she'd gotten involved with Joe. Stopping in the middle of housewares, she tried to face the truth of her pain.

She'd always feared Joe would come to his senses and realize she wasn't what he wanted or needed. She had known it would hurt, but she had thought she could at least salvage a fraction of her self-respect and pride. That could be accomplished by not seeing him. Since she was pregnant with his baby, she was hard-pressed to put her self-respect back together when she felt shredded every time she saw him.

His harsh distrust of her should have cured her of any attraction she held for him. Surely he had snuffed out any chance for love in her heart. She was cured of her secret, silly wishes.

She *knew* he viewed her as an obligation, and that knowledge upset her so much she wanted to scream. Her throat tightened, and she swallowed the urge even now.

She walked again, taking deep breaths to calm herself. Sometimes it was still hard to believe she'd gotten herself into this mess. She was the practical, careful, educated one. An unplanned pregnancy didn't seem possible. Even after suffering from morning sickness and hearing the baby's heartbeat, sometimes she still didn't quite believe she was pregnant.

Coming to a stop, she found herself in front of the baby department. She walked slowly toward a white crib decorated with colorful bumper pads of the sun, moon and stars. She wound the matching mobile and listened to the song, "When You Wish upon a Star." Marley thought of all the wishes her child would make and all she would try to make come true. She thought of all the secret wishes she'd had about Joe, and the sadness slipped in again.

"I have never seen a woman get so furious when she's just been offered a Cadillac," a too-familiar male voice said from behind her.

Marley's heart jumped like she'd received an injection of caffeine. She kept her eyes on the mobile. She didn't want to look at him. He wrecked her system even if her heart was cured.

"You're the psychologist. Take pity on me and explain this," he said, stepping beside her.

Watching him pick up a teddy bear from the crib, she felt a surge of emotion. She looked away. "Okay. Just for a moment pretend I'm the millionaire and you're not. You are pregnant with my baby. At first I didn't believe the baby was mine and I thought you were trying to *trick* me into marrying you."

Marley's blood pressure rose at the memory, but she went on. "Out of obligation, I'm offering to buy a new luxury car for you that you don't really want. How would you feel?"

Tossing the bear back into the crib, he crossed his arms over his chest. "If I'm going through this pregnancy stuff for nine months, I deserve a helluva lot more than a Cadillac."

Marley groaned and turned to walk away. "You're hopeless. You'll never get it."

Joe caught her arm and pulled her against him. "The problem with your little pretend game is that you've got a few of your facts twisted. One, I'm not offering to buy a new luxury car for you out of obligation. That little piece of tin you've got wouldn't protect you from a fender bender let alone a real accident."

Realization sank in. "Protection. You want to protect the baby."

"Right, and I want to protect the baby's mother." He turned her around, and the dangerous glint in his eyes made her feel like she'd just stepped into quicksand. He wrapped his hands around her wrists like handcuffs and tugged her too close. "This isn't about obligation, Marley. Something you don't *get* is that you've been important to me since the day we met. That hasn't changed, and it never will."

Right in the middle of Wal-Mart, Joe lowered his head and took her mouth in a kiss she was certain created havoc in the shoe department and ladies lingerie, if not the entire universe. Marley locked her knees, tried to lock her heart and swore she was cured.

Ten

He'd lost her.

He knew the exact moment it had happened. He knew the exact words he'd said. He had let his anger and confusion talk for him.

And he'd lost her.

Joe walked the length of his too-quiet den, aware of Dixie's curious gaze. He suspected his retriever had decided her human was a couple of dog biscuits short of a full box. Joe would have to agree.

He didn't want to go to his bedroom anymore. Even though it had been weeks since she'd slept with him, he still reached for her in the night. Every morning he woke up with empty hands, feeling vacant and hollow.

Marley had filled him up and made him feel as if he'd found his place in the universe. In her gentle but firm way, she'd forced him to see himself differently. He should have held her so she'd never gone away. He should have cherished her.

Instead he'd lost her.

He sat down on his couch, planted his elbows on his knees and stared into space. He couldn't even go out on the balcony anymore. Halfway up the spiral stairs, he was deluged with visuals that stopped him. Marley with her eyes full of love and laughter, her arms wrapped around him. Marley feeding a muffin to him and playfully biting him when he returned the favor. Marley full of passion, completely open and trusting, taking him all the way inside her.

He had to get her back. He rubbed his face in frustration. He had to get her back, but he didn't know how.

Hearing Marley's laughter behind the partly closed door of her office, Joe grinned and looked through the doorway. Marley stood between Lynn and a man whose hands were on her slightly protruding belly.

"There," Marley said, her eyes round with excitement. She looked innocent and sexy at the same time. "Did you feel that?"

Lynn squinted in concentration. "I dunno. What do you think, Kevin? How do you tell the difference between the baby moving and indigestion?"

"It moved again!" Marley said.

"I felt that," Kevin murmured, moving his hand slightly over her abdomen.

Seeing another man's hand on Marley sent a tidal wave of possessiveness thrumming through his blood. He was struck with the shocking, primitive urge to break the guy's hand. Sucking in a quick, sharp breath, he shook his head. "Maybe your shirt is getting in the way," Kevin suggested.

"Think so?"

Marley looked as if she were actually considering lifting her shirt for him to paw her. *In another lifetime,* Joe thought, swearing under his breath as he strode through the door.

Marley's gaze flew to meet his. Her eyes brightened for a full moment, making him feel like he had the world by the tail. The moment passed too quickly, however, and the sparkle dimmed as if she remembered she wasn't supposed to feel so strongly about him. Joe clenched his fist in frustration.

"The baby's moving," Marley told him. "It's just little flutters right now. Kevin and Lynn wanted to feel it, too...." She gave a little shrug.

Joe moved toward her, holding her gaze. "I'd like to feel it," he told her. "Is it still moving?"

She nodded and guided his hand to her abdomen. Joe watched Kevin's hand fall away and felt something inside him ease. The room had a hushed quality. Joe closed his eyes to concentrate and felt a gentle stirring from inside Marley.

He opened his eyes in astonishment. "I felt it. That's the baby?" he asked.

Her grin stretched from ear to ear. "Yes. Would you say soccer or gymnastics?"

"Both," he said decisively.

Kevin cleared his throat. "Or maybe you've got a kick-boxing champion." He slid Joe a look of challenge, then turned to Marley. "Let me know about Saturday night. I left my number on your desk. Okay?"

Looking vaguely uncomfortable, Marley nodded. "Okay."

Joe wondered if Marley would consider wearing a sign around her neck that she was off-limits. He wondered if Kevin would quit hitting on Marley if his tongue were wrapped around his throat a couple of times.

Lynn hung around after Kevin left. "Nice rear end," she said to Marley at the same time she shot Joe a sly look. "Looks like one of Denver's top-ten most-wanted bachelors has got a little competition."

"Lynn," Marley said in a warning tone.

Lynn just smiled and drummed her fingers on a piece of paper on Marley's desk. "No worry. A little competition's a very healthy thing. Isn't that what capitalists say, Joe?" She sauntered out the door. "Have a nice evening."

Joe nodded and clenched his fist in his pocket.

"You too, Lynn," Marley said, then closed the door behind her and sighed. She glanced at Joe. "She's crazy."

"Maybe. How long has Kevin been coming around?"

"He's one of the teaching assistants," she said with a shrug. "He's just a nice guy."

"How long has he been after you?"

"That might be too strong a way of putting it," she said and laughed self-consciously. "His interest is flattering, considering I feel about as sexually exciting as white bread."

Incredulous, he asked, "Why?"

"I've been nauseated for six weeks. Now, I'm losing my waist. I'm in the *fat* stage," she said.

"No, you're not. You're just starting to show."

She shook her head and smiled. "You're kind."

He swore under his breath. "You have no idea how sexy you are."

Her cheeks bloomed with color, and she lifted her hand in protest. "You really don't need to try to make me feel better. I—"

Joe pulled her against him and kissed her until she softened in his arms. He slid one of his hands up her side and nuzzled her ear. "I can tell your breasts are fuller, and I bet they're more sensitive," he muttered, brushing his fingers on the outer edge of her breast. He could see the unbidden, arousing sign of her excitement in her peaked nipples. He grazed one with his fingertip, and she went perfectly still.

He wanted to go further. He wanted to put his mouth on her and taste her with his tongue. He wanted to take off her clothes and make her his in every way. But he sensed her ambivalence. Her opposing feelings were strong, and he couldn't take her when she was divided. He wanted her totally open to him.

Reining in his need and the desperation that stung him at unexpected moments, he bided his time and lowered his hand to her waist. "You're more curvy than ever. Men look at you and see a ripe, sexual woman. Your waist is still there, but the baby's growing more. Do you know how much it turns me on knowing you've got my baby growing inside you?''

Her breath came out in a soft gasp. ''That's hard for me to believe. You said you didn't want—''

He covered her mouth, unwilling to hear his foolish words played back to him. ''I know better now.''

Marley looked up into his gaze with questioning blue eyes. She tentatively lifted her hand to his chin. ''Do you? Do you really know better now?''

''Yes,'' he told her, hearing the rough need in his voice. ''Let me show you.''

Marley closed her eyes and shuddered. She leaned into him, and he felt the heady anticipation of victory. But she pulled away. Her trembling hands offered little consolation. He wanted her, all of her.

She stepped back and looked away. ''What brings you here tonight?''

''I need to talk with you,'' he said.

She must have heard the somber note in his voice because she glanced at him quizzically. ''About what?''

''I'd rather talk somewhere else. After dinner at my house?'' He wanted to push. Despite repeated invitations, she hadn't been inside his house since she'd gone to Cheyenne.

''Why don't we eat Chinese at my house? My treat,'' she said with a tentative smile.

''I'll take care of it,'' he automatically said.

''No,'' she said, surprising him with her firmness. ''Just because you're Mr. Moneybags doesn't mean you get to pay all the time.''

Joe blinked. A woman paying instead of him? It was unprecedented.

"You look like I smacked you."

Struggling with the prospect of her paying, he shook his head at his loss for words. "I'm not sure what to say."

She grabbed her jacket from a hook. "How about 'Thank you. I'll take Szechwan cabbage'?"

There she went, turning him around again. He dipped his head. "Okay. Thank you. I'll take sesame chicken."

"Meet you at my house," she said with a smile.

An hour later as they finished the last of the Chinese takeout, Marley covered her stomach and groaned. "I can't believe I ate that much. Just a couple of weeks ago, I could barely keep down soda crackers."

Joe watched her through hooded eyes as he drank his bottled beer. "The baby's going through a growth spurt."

"Or I am," she said wryly, foreseeing a demanding fitness routine in her future next summer. "But I'll deal with that later. One thing at a time. Maternity clothes first. I'm thinking about the nursery, but I don't think I'll actually *do* anything about it until the last trimester."

"The nursery," he said, shaking his head. "It hadn't crossed my mind until that day we were in Wal-Mart."

His gaze caught hers, and she knew he was remembering the same moment when he'd kissed her. Marley took a slow, deep breath. His effect on her was still so powerful it was difficult for Marley to keep her head straight. Even in her office, she'd wanted more from him, with him. But she couldn't have more, she kept telling herself. There *was* no more.

"How does a shrink decorate a nursery?" he asked, bringing her back to reality.

Marley looked down her nose at him and tossed the cardboard cartons into the trash. "I plan to use a scientific approach with the color scheme and make the baby's surroundings evoke an atmosphere of security and comfort."

He looked at her skeptically. "Scientific approach with the color scheme?"

"Yes," she said, returning to her seat across from him at the small kitchen table. "Studies have been conducted to find the most soothing color."

"I can hardly wait. What is it?"

Marley's lips twitched at the tinge of dread in his voice. He'll croak, she thought. "Bubble gum pink."

His eyes widened in horror. "You're kidding."

"Not at all. Studies performed in prisons revealed that the color bubble gum pink had the most calming effect on prisoners."

"Prisoners!" He rubbed a hand over his face. "What if you have a boy? You're not gonna make his room *pink,* are you? His buddies will call him a sissy."

"Do you have any idea how sexist you sound?"

"Hey, you're the shrink. You want your son to be scarred for life because you painted his room *pink?*" he asked, emphasizing the last word with disgust.

"There might be another choice."

"Yellow."

She shook her head. "No. Studies have shown that babies cry longer and harder when they're in nurseries painted yellow. I'm thinking green. Green is supposed to have a soothing, comforting effect."

Joe looked visibly relieved. "I'm not surprised. Why do you think they made money green?"

She laughed, rolling her eyes. "Sometimes I can't believe the way your mind works."

"Back at ya," he said with the same grin that made her heart flip. "What else are you going to put in the nursery?"

"I want to get one of those things that sounds like a human heartbeat, and I think I want to decorate the room with a baby animal motif. I saw this cute Noah's Ark wallpaper border and I want music boxes, several of them—" She paused, tempering her excitement. "It's not very practical. If I were being practical, I would focus more on something the baby can grow with."

Joe put his hand over hers. "You can do that later, can't you?"

A rush of emotions welled inside her at the sight of his hand. His hand meant strength and passion to her. His was the hand of her lover. Desperation pulled at her. She closed her eyes for a second, then opened them. Would she ever get past him?

She remembered he had said he wanted to talk. "What did you want to tell me?"

His eyes darkened and he paused for a moment. "You need to know that if I should die or become incapacitated, there is a trust set up for you and the baby.''

Her chest tightened at the thought of Joe dying. ''What are you talking about?''

''It's called a living trust. If I die or become incapacitated, then you and the baby will be taken care of. You'll receive a monthly check, and the child will receive a chunk on his or her eighteenth birthday, a stipend until age twenty-five. Then, at age thirty, he or she will get the rest.''

Marley tried to absorb the details, but she was stuck on the thought of Joe being hurt. ''Do you really think this is necessary?''

''For my peace of mind, it is. We also need to talk about guardians if you and I should die before the child grows up. I spent half my childhood scared spitless my mom would die and I would end up in a foster home.''

Her mind whirling, Marley shook her head. ''How could I have missed this? I've been thinking about prenatal vitamins and nursery decor.''

''You would have thought of it eventually,'' he said with a shrug. ''I went today...''

Marley waited for the reason why he went today, but Joe said nothing more. ''Why today?''

He narrowed his eyes and cocked his head to one side. ''I guess you could say it's an anniversary. My mom died on this day ten years ago.''

Marley felt the explanation like a blow. ''Oh.'' She lowered her head into her hand. ''I imagine that stirs up all kinds of memories for you.''

The barest trace of a smile lifted his mouth and he

nodded. "Not all of them are bad. I remember one time she tried to teach me to fish, but she hated the idea of using worms, so we used baloney. When we caught one, she screamed so loud you would have thought we'd caught a ten-pound tuna. It was a small, ugly catfish."

Marley saw the range of emotions ebb and flow in his dark eyes, and she felt the same tug and pull inside her. "Do you look like her?"

He met her gaze. "I have her eyes."

"What was her personality like?"

"I don't know what she was like before she had me. I remember wishing she would smile more, laugh more. She seemed serious, and tired most of the time."

Marley thought about that little boy and what a burden he must have felt he was. A lump formed in her throat.

"I don't want that for you," he said.

She frowned. "You don't want what?"

"I don't want you to lose your laughter. I don't want you to stop smiling. I don't want you tired all the time."

The power in his gaze shook her. "I'm not like your mother, Joe. I'll be fine."

"You're damn right you will be." He stood and began to pace the small length of her kitchen. "I haven't worked out all the details, but I'm also going to set up a self-sustaining bond where you'll receive a check once a month."

Confused, she watched his stern expression. "That's the living trust, right?"

"No. You'll receive this check while I'm alive."

Realization hit her, and she stood. "No. I told you I don't expect—"

"I will support my child," he told her with a finality that would have set stone.

Marley sighed. "You didn't choose this."

"Neither did you."

They stared at each other for a long moment.

Joe's lips twitched in irony. "My lawyer tells me I can set this up any way I want. When I told him you wouldn't marry me, he said I could stipulate a hundred thousand dollar bonus if you married me. If I thought it would work, I would do it, Marley."

Sadness sliced through her. He still didn't get it. "I don't want your money."

His jaw tightened and he turned away, shoving his hands into his pockets. "I know."

His aloneness permeated her. She hated the thought of him suffering, and from all her education, she knew she couldn't fix it. Maybe she didn't want to fix it, though, she thought. Maybe she just wanted to ease the pain. Maybe she just wanted to be close to him.

Marley touched his arm and felt his tension vibrate through her. She felt him take a breath, then he covered her hand with his and turned to look at her.

"I still want you," he said in a rough voice.

Her heart twisted. What could she say? It will pass? Did she really want it to pass?

She swallowed over the lump in her throat. "I don't want you to feel alone."

He pulled her into the circle of his arms. "Then stay with me."

Marley sighed. "That will cause other problems."

"None that I can see," he said, and lowered his mouth to brush his lips against hers.

She breathed in his scent and felt her good sense slipping away. She stretched her hands around his neck. "Oh, Joe, what are we doing?" she whispered.

"Just kissing, Marley."

His tongue teased past her lips and to Marley it was much more than kissing. Her body ached for his touch, and her hands longed to bring him pleasure. She wanted to take and be taken, by him.

She pulled away and ducked her head beneath his chin, inhaling quick breaths to clear her mind, but breathing his scent kept her feeling cloudy. "I want to be with you, but I'm not sure this is best."

He gave a rough, humorless chuckle. "This has always been the best. This has always been right." Hooking his thumb under her chin, he urged her to meet his gaze. "Did you really think it would go away?"

Marley recalled that horrible conversation when she'd told him about the baby. She'd lost all hope. "Yes, I did."

Eleven

Marley bit down on her carrot stick in frustration. Although the sun was shining in the mile-high city, her discontent swirled inside her like rain clouds. Lynn had coaxed her into an extended lunch, promising it would improve her mood.

Lynn joined her at the small café table and held up her fingers in the sign of the cross. "Don't look at my salad. You'll make it wilt."

Marley gave a slight smile. "Sorry. I was just thinking."

"About Daddy Warbucks," Lynn said, digging into her salad. "Lots to think about. I can't believe you haven't hit the sack with him since August."

"It would mess up my head."

"Like it's not messed up now?" Lynn asked.

"You have such a warm, gentle way about you,

Lynn. Are you sure you shouldn't go into a different occupation like debt collection?''

"Deflecting the attention from you to me isn't going to work. What are you going to do with Joe?''

Marley bit into another carrot and thought about it. "I don't know. When I look at him, I automatically think of self-help books for women. *Men Afraid of Commitment, Ten Ways Women Mess Up Their Lives, Women Who Love Too Much,* and *The Wizard of Oz.*''

Lynn wrinkled her face in confusion. *"The Wizard of Oz?''*

"Tin man," Marley told her. "You know, the one who needs a heart?''

Lynn shrugged. "Well, Joe's definitely got a heart. Look at everything he's trying to do to make your pregnancy easier. If you needed him, he would be there for you like that," she said, snapping her fingers.

"Maybe," Marley said, her doubts still a source of darkness. "I haven't seen much of him at night lately.''

"Do you think he's going out with another woman?''

Marley's stomach sank to her feet. "I don't know. He could be, but it's more likely that he's working. I can't help wondering if he still blames me for the baby.'' She thought about what bothered her most and put down her carrot stick. "He never told me he loved me.''

There, she'd said it. She should have confided it

earlier. Marley knew better than most that a shared pain was easier to bear. She let out a sigh.

"You mean he never used the words," Lynn corrected. "Because from the outside looking in, it looks like he's screaming it."

Lynn's words resonated inside her. More truth, but she found no peace in it. More confusion, because she'd resolved that she couldn't have what she wanted or needed with Joe. "I don't want to get caught in that cycle of wanting something from him, yet not being willing to ask for it. It appalls me, but I can't *ask* him to tell me he loves me. I would rather shave my head."

Lynn cocked her head to one side. "I'm not sure that would solve your dilemma. Listen, this is none of my business," Lynn said, then gave a dry laugh. "Of course that's never stopped me before. Joe doesn't have a doctorate in psychology. He's a G.I. Joe type emotionally, a man of action," she said in a mock melodramatic tone. "You might not want to count him out. He knew a good thing when he found you, and it looks like he's doing his damnedest to keep you. You're going to have to decide if you want to be kept or not."

"Trust me," Joe said.

Marley groaned as he tied the handkerchief over her eyes. "Why does this feel like déjà vu?"

"It's different," he assured her. "Trust me."

"I've always hated it when people said that to me. My mother said 'Trust me' after my tonsils were taken out, and the first bite of ice cream had yucky medicine in it.''

"No ice cream or medicine tonight," he said, putting the car into gear and accelerating.

"My sister said 'Trust me, there are no jellyfish' and I got stung.''

Joe snickered. "There are no jellyfish. We're land-locked." He hesitated. "Tell me, how long have you had difficulty trusting people? You mentioned your mother," he said with an atrocious German accent.

"You do a rotten Sigmund Freud," she grumbled. She wasn't fond of her crankiness, but her usual pick-me-ups were leaving her flat. She was in the second trimester of her pregnancy, approaching the holiday season, physically terrific, energy level at an all-time high, the baby was great. She should be flying.

Marley felt like The Grinch before Christmas.

She wanted a clear head, an inner serenity, peace. Joe lightly hooked his hand behind the nape of her neck, and she felt firecrackers go off. It was almost enough to make her take up swearing.

"Is this a mind thing? The blindfold?''

He gently squeezed her. "Actually it's more of a sexual thing. Is that what you meant?''

She felt her blood heat. "Not exactly.''

"Hypnotism?" he guessed. "I hadn't thought of it. Let's start with something simple. Repeat after me. I want to drive a Volvo. I want to drive the car with the best safety record. I want to ditch my Honda Civic and drive the Volvo that Joe will give me.''

Marley laughed despite her mood.

He gave a long-suffering sigh. "It won't work if you don't follow my instructions. Repeat after me."

"I love my Honda. I love my Honda. I love my—"

He put his hand over her mouth. "Hush! After all the trouble I went to to find a smaller car."

"With a bigger price tag," Marley added, her reply muffled against his palm.

He gave another long-suffering sigh, and Marley felt the car make a turn. "I never thought I'd say this, but, darling, I believe you're obsessed with money."

"Me!" she shrieked.

"Yes, you. Didn't your mother ever teach you the proper way to accept a gift. Say thank you and shut up," he told her with a grin in his voice.

"My mother was too busy singing The Beatles' song as my lullaby."

"Which one was that?" he asked her, pulling to a stop.

" 'Money Can't Buy Me Love,' " she said, smiling at the memory.

"True, but it can buy just about everything else. Okay, my little democrat. Time for the surprise."

She heard him get out of the car and open her door.

"Take my hand," he said, and she felt an odd sense of anticipation.

"Are you sure this isn't ice cream?" she asked, almost wishing it was. She had the crazy feeling that something momentous was about to occur.

"Not this time."

As soon as she stepped out of his car, she knew she was in his garage. Her stomach twisted as memories flooded her. She'd avoided his house because she'd left so many of her secret wishes and dreams there.

He led her through the door, and she heard the click of Dixie's feet on the tile floor. A moment later she felt the dog brush against her. Murmuring a soft greeting, Marley bent down to pet her soft fur.

Joe wrapped his hand more securely around hers and led her up the stairs.

Reluctantly she dragged her feet after him. "I don't know about this, Joe. I don't think this is a good idea. Last time—"

"This is different," he said, then muttered, "unfortunately."

She held her breath as they walked past his bedroom door. A sliver of curiosity overrode her tension. "What are you—"

He pulled her through a doorway and stepped away from her, flicking on a lamp. She lifted her hands to the handkerchief.

"Wait a minute."

Marley stood in the darkness and waited.

A winding sound followed by sweet, tinkling music broke the hushed expectancy.

Marley listened and smiled. "'Twinkle, Twinkle Little Star,'" she said, easily identifying the song from her childhood. She lifted her hands again to the handkerchief.

"Not yet," Joe said.

Another tinkling melody joined the first.

She listened carefully. "'Brahms's Lullaby.'"

"Name that music box tune," he said, and still another tinkling tune filled the other.

The combination of the different songs could have been discordant and confusing, but for Marley it was a sweet mingling of memories. Tears came to her eyes. "'Talk to the Animals,'" she said.

She felt Joe at her side. He pulled away the handkerchief, and she blinked. A dozen images hit her at once. Noah's Ark wallpaper border. A lamp with porcelain baby animals rested on top of a light-stained wooden chest of drawers. A Jenny Lind crib with green bumper pads and crib sheet.

Her heart tightened. He'd listened to her every word, her every wish. She glanced beside the crib to the large kid-sized mural of baby animals painted on the wall.

"I can't believe you did this," she managed over the lump in her throat, almost afraid to look at Joe. "When did you have time?"

"At night," he said, jingling the keys in his pocket. "I've had a lot of time at night lately. Did I get everything right?"

She felt his gaze and her eyes burned more intensely. "It's perfect. I can't believe it. It's beautiful," she said, and moved closer to touch the puffy baby animals on the mobile. "I don't know what to say."

"Say you'll move in," he said in a low, rough voice.

Her heart jumped into her throat, and she swung to stare at him. "Oh, Joe."

She could see evidence of the battle warring inside him. Pain, determination and a guardedness permeated him. He narrowed his eyes. "You don't have to share my bed. You can have your own room."

Shock jolted her. She stumbled for words. "Is...is that what you want?"

His gaze darkened. "Don't ask me what I want, Marley," he said in a dangerous tone.

Irresistibly drawn despite the danger, she stepped closer. "Why?"

He lifted his hand to touch her hair, then drew back as if he was trying to restrain himself.

The possibility hurt her.

"Don't ask me what I want, unless you really want to know."

Since the first time she'd met Joe, she'd always wanted to *know* him. The storminess in his dark eyes called to her. Marley had always loved thunderstorms, the power, the passion. She felt as if she were standing on the edge of a cliff over water. If she stepped off the edge, would she ever be able to swim back to shore?

She took a deep breath and tentatively touched his face. "I want to know."

He put his hand over hers and slid his hand behind her back to draw her against him. She immediately felt his arousal.

"Do you feel what you do to me?" he asked her, rubbing his rough cheek against her palm. "I want you. I want you in my bed every night, and I want to make love to you every morning. I want to see you and feel you."

He moved his hand down to cup her bottom, rocking her against his hardness. He lowered his forehead to rest against hers. "You're not going to like this, but you've made me a greedy man. I want to own you."

It was a sexist comment, but the way he said it sounded more like need. The way he said it sounded as if he wanted to keep her. *For how long?* she wondered, then echoed the question out loud. "For how long?"

"As long as you'll have me." As if he couldn't hold back any longer, he tugged her dress upward and plunged his hands beneath her panties to caress her bare skin.

Marley shuddered.

"Let me have you," he said in a voice that made her bones melt. "I've dreamed of you."

He took her mouth, and Marley was spinning. His confession was too primitive and strong for her to deny him or herself.

"I've missed you," he muttered as he unzipped her dress and sent it to pool at her feet. Her bra followed.

His mouth worked magic over her. He kissed aside her doubts and stoked her passion into a raging flame. Aching for him, she unbuttoned his shirt and pushed it aside, then started on his belt.

"I've missed you, too," she whispered, and all she wanted was to show him.

Her inhibitions blew away like a Wyoming wind, and she took his mouth the way he'd taken hers. She suckled his tongue deep into hers and tasted him. She had the illicit, uneasy sense that she couldn't get enough of him, that he couldn't get enough of her.

She touched his bare chest and skimmed her mouth down his neck to his hard chest. She rubbed her tongue over his nipples, making them harden.

He shuddered and swore. ''Marley,'' he said with a hint of warning in his voice.

Heedless of his admonition, she urged him on. She felt as if she'd been without water and this was her first drink. She was desperate to taste, driven to consume.

He pulled her back up to kiss his mouth and while his chest gently abraded the sensitive tips of her breasts, his hands took an erotic journey between her thighs. He found her swollen and wet and stroked the tiny bead of sensation until she was quivering in response. He plunged his finger inside her and Marley cried out.

Suddenly nothing was enough.

With her mouth, she glided down his body, taking his passion and giving hers. She kissed her way down his abdomen, dipping her tongue into his navel.

''Marley,'' he said again, in a rough voice.

She felt him twine his fingers through her hair. Any sane woman would have stopped, but Marley was past sanity. She moved her mouth in one continuous motion down his abdomen to his hard masculinity.

He was huge and swollen, and she was driven.

She took him into her mouth and made love to him.

He swore again and again, but it sounded like a

lover's pleading, and Marley couldn't stop even when she tasted his essence.

Joe flinched and pushed her mouth from him. He shifted her shoulders and she caught the honey of his passion on her breasts and abdomen, claiming her, marking her as *his*. Here, in this room he'd made for her, for their baby, it was the most powerfully erotic experience of her life, and Marley began to tremble.

"Oh, sweetheart, come here," he said, pulling her up in his arms. "Come here."

He carried her down the hall to the master bath and turned on the jets to the shower.

"I don't think I can stand," she confessed.

He gazed down at her. "I'll hold you."

And he did. He stepped into the warm spray and held her and washed her. His tenderness moved her to tears. Marley tried to hide them from him. He matched the power of her passion, but could he possibly match the strength of her emotion?

Joe set her down on his bed as if she were fine china and stared at her. She was wrapped in a towel, and he preferred her nude, but he wouldn't complain. At last she was here again. Her blond hair, tousled and damp, contrasted sharply with the midnight blue sheets and quilt. That was part of what she was to him, he thought, the light in the darkness.

He noticed her red-rimmed eyes, but was unsure if that was good or bad, so he didn't say anything. He only knew he wanted her to stay.

Feeling as if he was walking through a minefield,

he stuck to the basics. "Would you like something to drink?"

"Yes, please. Juice," she said so softly no one would believe she had taken him by storm just moments ago.

At the minibar, he poured her orange juice and a glass of wine for himself, then joined her on the bed. He watched her down the juice in record time and raised his eyebrows. "A little thirsty?"

She shook her head. "A lot thirsty."

"More?" he asked.

She hesitated, and her gaze slid down to his chest, then back to his eyes. "Yes. More, but not juice."

His heart stopped at the bold request in her gaze. Could she possibly want him half as much as he wanted her? He took a quick gulp of his wine then put both their glasses on the bedside table.

She unwrapped her towel and he drank in the sight of her naked and growing with his child. Her breasts were swollen, her nipples dusky and large. His body hardened with want and he lowered his head to take the tip into his mouth. He loved the sensation of her nipple transforming to a firm bud against his tongue. He gently grazed his teeth against her.

She gasped and rubbed her thighs against his.

"You like that?" he muttered, licking her.

"Yes-s-s," she said.

"If I keep going," he said, drawing deeply on her, then tugging with his tongue between each word. "I think I could almost make you—"

Marley stiffened and cried out. "Oh, my— Oh-h-h-h." She gave a long, breathless moan.

Unwilling to let her catch her breath or sanity, he slid his hand between her thighs and found her wet and swollen for him. Returning his mouth to her breasts, he played with her, plunging his finger inside her and rubbing his thumb over her hot spot.

She peaked in fits and starts, again and again. She cried out his name and it was like music to him. His need for her was a drumbeat in his head that wouldn't go away.

She pushed his hand away and stroked him. He wanted to thrust inside her, hard and full, all the way. He wanted to take her so that she would never forget him, so that she would never forget she belonged to him.

He swore under his breath. "I don't want to hurt you."

Her eyes heavy-lidded and sultry with passion, she shook her head. "You won't."

But Joe didn't trust himself. She may have sent him over the edge just moments before, but the cavern grew deeper each time. He wanted as much of her as he could take.

With trembling hands, he rolled them over so that she straddled him. He watched her eyes widen in sensuous surprise.

Then Marley lifted slightly and took him inside her. Sweet, tight, wet. It was the sexiest sight he'd ever seen. Marley, naked with her hair spilling over her plump breasts and enlarged nipples, her belly rounded with their child. Her blue eyes were fastened on him as if he were her world.

He almost exploded then, but he gritted his teeth together and reined himself in.

Then he saw the expression on her face. *Not enough, never enough.* She began to move, a voluptuous undulation that milked his sex and sanity.

Joe fought against his release. He wanted this moment to last forever. Somewhere beyond the roaring in his ears, he thought he heard her whisper, "I love you." And he tumbled over the edge again.

Throughout the night they would sleep, then he would awaken and reach for her again, reminding her that she belonged with him, reassuring himself that she was here with him. Just before dawn they made love again, and Joe drifted into a dreamless sleep.

When he awoke again, he was alone and the place where she'd slept had cooled. He heard the faint strains of a music box beyond his closed door. Quickly rising from bed, Joe pulled on a pair of jeans and called out her name, "Marley?"

"In here," she said a moment later, hesitation in her tone. "In the nursery."

He strode down the hall to find her wearing his robe and standing in the middle of the room as she listened to the song. Her pensive posture gave him a trickle of unease.

She gave a sad smile. "You didn't play one of the songs yesterday. 'Edelweiss' is one of my favorites."

"I couldn't find one about daffodils," he said, referring to his long-ago comparison of Marley to a daffodil.

Her smile faded. "It's beautiful. They're all beautiful."

Joe sucked in a quick, sharp breath. He heard a *but* coming like a freight train, and he knew in his gut it wasn't going to be good.

"Are you game for a trip to the balcony?"

She looked away. "Not this morning. I—"

"You want breakfast." He made it a statement instead of a question.

"No." She met his gaze and what he saw in her eyes ripped him in half. She was scared.

He clenched his jaw and stepped closer to her. "What's going on?"

Marley sighed and shook her head. "I don't know. I'm not sure we—" She hesitated, lifting her hands, clearly searching for words. "Last night, we might not—"

He was hurt and angry with himself for giving a damn whether she left or not. "This isn't some kind of lame morning-after regret, is it, Marley? We've known each other too long and too well for that, wouldn't you say?"

She winced as if his words stung. "There's nothing lame about this morning. There was nothing lame about last night. Last night was beautiful."

"Then what is it, Marley? What's the problem?" he demanded.

"I d-don't know," she said, faltering. She closed her eyes, then opened them. "I don't know if we can be what each of us needs for the long run."

Frustration raised the hackles on his skin. Past

hurt, past angry, he confronted her. "What's wrong with me? What's missing?"

Her eyes rounded in surprise. "Nothing."

"There must be something. I'm too tall, too short, too dark—"

"No, you're extremely attractive and you know it. This isn't about physical characteristics."

He lifted his eyebrows. "Then it must be my character, personality. I'm too moody. I have too much money," he said sarcastically, feeling like a bull in a china shop. Right now it seemed as if he could do nothing right, or say nothing right.

"No," she said, then rolled her head in a circle. "Yes, you're moody, but I like your moodiness. I just don't know if we can make it last."

"What is it going to take to convince you that I want to marry you? You and the baby belong here with me. I can provide for you financially. I can—"

Her face drawn tight from tension, Marley lifted her hand. "This isn't about money."

He stared at her and abhorred the defeat that gripped him. "You're right. This isn't about money. This is about playing it safe. The reason you don't want to stay with me is because I'm not safe."

Twelve

Joe took Marley home, then returned to his house. The silence that greeted him made him acutely aware of his loneliness. He swore as he walked across the Italian tile in his kitchen. He'd never had a problem with loneliness until Marley blasted into his life. He'd been just fine on his path to becoming a billionaire.

A lonely billionaire.

He swore again, thinking of the nursery and how he'd foolishly hoped it would work some magic and bring Marley back.

Unable to sit, he paced to the counter and shuffled through the past few days' mail again. He pulled out the letter from Stan Michaels. In his physician's scrawl, Stan thanked Joe for the wedding gift and chided him for not attending his recent wedding to Jenna Jean. Joe shook his head. He still couldn't believe those two had actually gotten married. They had fought like cats and dogs when they were kids.

Joe looked at the last line of Stan's note. "Come visit us anytime. Standing invitation."

He tapped the paper in his hand thoughtfully. Marley was leaving to visit her family back east for the holidays. Although meeting her family might have been as much fun as going to the dentist, he wished he was important enough to her that she would have invited him.

He wasn't. A too-familiar hurt burned through him, and he tried to shake it off.

She'd suggested they spend some time apart thinking about what each of them really wanted from the other. Sounded like more shrink rap to Joe. As far as he could see, when Marley spent too much time thinking, it caused a helluva lot of trouble for him.

He rubbed his face in frustration. The Christmas holidays were staring him in the face. Joe viewed the coming season with as much anticipation as he would welcome a recession. His longtime pal, Sam, was going down to Vegas. Joe had been there, done that, and didn't want to do it again. He would receive plenty of invitations he had no interest in accepting. He could work through the holiday and pretend it didn't exist. *Like Scrooge.*

He scowled and glanced at the note from Stan.

Well, hell. Maybe it was time to be a Bad Boy again.

* * *

"To the Bad Boys, who got their start on Cherry Lane," Stan Michaels, now an orthopedic physician, made the toast with a mischievous grin. "May our mission never die."

"To raise hell wherever we go," Ben said, and downed his beer.

Joe took a long swallow from his own bottle, then wiped his mouth. It was the day before Christmas Eve and the rowdy bar was jam-packed. The music was loud, the company great. If he was lucky, the combination of the noise and beer would chase Marley Fuller from his mind, if only for a few hours.

"I technically didn't get my start on Cherry Lane," he pointed out to the guys.

"We knew where you lived," Stan said, and ordered another round from the waitress. "You were close enough."

"Plus you were great in math," Ben said.

Surprised, Joe looked from one grown-up Bad Boy to the other. "Did you know about my dad, too?"

"That he didn't exist?" Ben said. "Yep, we knew."

Joe sat back in his seat and shook his head. He gave a wry laugh. "And I thought I covered all that up."

"You did for a while," Stan said. "But we were curious—"

"Nosy as hell," Ben corrected bluntly. "Stan and I followed you home one day."

"My little wife tells me you're not living in the

same kind of neighborhood in Denver,'' Stan said with a knowing glance.

Joe grinned at the way Stan described Roanoke's Assistant Commonwealth Attorney as his *little wife.* ''She's right. It's my Graceland in the Rockies minus the green shag carpeting growing up the wall and down from the ceiling.''

''Steak restaurants,'' Ben said with approval. ''You make money *and* get a great meal.''

Uncomfortable being the focus of attention, Joe shrugged. ''It pays the bills. What about you, *Bad* Ben? I thought you would be the Easy Rider of the nineties.''

Ben still looked like a nonconformist to the bone. The back of his hair almost touched his shoulders. He wore a black leather jacket that would have done James Dean proud. Add his don't-give-a-damn attitude and an earring in one ear, and he looked like every father's worst nightmare.

Stan snickered. ''Ben is now a stable, tax-paying member of society.''

''Quit rubbing it in, Stanley,'' Ben said with a scowl.

''Ben owns and operates the top foreign-car dealership and repair shop in Roanoke,'' Stan continued.

''But I still drive a Harley, I'm not married, will never be, and I don't have any kids.'' Ben slid a superior glance over Stan. ''I'm not married and mowing the lawn on Saturdays.''

''Hey, I can't help it if you can't find a woman

who makes life in suburbia worth the trouble,'' Stan said.

"Touché. Jenna Jean's worth the trouble. But I've always said I like to pack light. That doesn't include a wife.'' Ben turned to Joe. "What about you? Have you found the dream woman? You ready to make some heirs?''

Joe set down his beer. Until now he'd enjoyed the evening. For a few hours he'd been able to put Marley partly from his mind. She was never out of sight, but he was drowning his frustration in beer and happy Bad Boy memories.

"I found someone,'' he finally said. "I don't know if it's gonna work out.''

Stan raised his eyebrows. "Why not?''

Joe shrugged. "Stupid stuff. She hates my money.''

Ben choked on his beer. "You're joking. I've never met a woman who didn't enjoy money. Hell, if that's the problem, then toss her back into the ring and find one who loves your money.''

The idea didn't appeal to Joe. Now that he'd found a woman who loved him for himself, he wouldn't settle for less. "That's not the only problem.''

"What else?''

"She's a vegetarian,'' Joe told him, wondering why he was avoiding the main issues. "And a shrink. And probably a democrat.''

Stan chuckled. "Sounds interesting.''

Joe sighed. "Plus, she's pregnant.''

The two men gaped at him.

"My baby," he said. "It was a surprise. We had a disagreement when she told me."

Realization crossed both men's faces.

"Disagreement," Ben said. "You screwed up, right?"

"Uh-huh," Joe said.

"On a scale of one to ten, how bad did you screw up?"

"Oh, about twenty," Joe said, and started on his next beer.

Ben cringed. "Ouch. You want her back?"

"Yep." *Either that, or shoot me.*

"Then you've come to the right place. Stan the Man had to jump through a few hoops to get Jenna Jean." Ben stood and shrugged his shoulder toward the bar. "While you domestic types talk, I'll head off Cindy Gillian. She's prowling in this direction."

"Remember what I said about women with police records," Stan said.

"Yeah, yeah. But the question is can she ride?" Ben said with a sly grin.

Joe remembered Ben's mantra that he wouldn't date a girl unless she could ride a motorcycle. "Is he serious?"

"Rarely," Stan said.

"What about the rest of the guys? Nail 'em Nick, Tex, Kevin." He closed his eyes, searching his mind for names and faces. "Spider?"

Stan sipped his beer. "A few of them came to the surprise birthday party Jenna had for me. Nick is a civil attorney in Richmond."

"No kidding." Joe remembered the scrawny, scrappy kid.

Stan shook his head and grinned. "Nope. Kevin's in the Navy. Tex is somewhere in Texas, and we couldn't find Spider." He clinked his beer bottle against Joe's. "Nobody was surprised to hear you had made it big. We all missed seeing you at the party and the wedding."

"Work," Joe muttered, an odd feeling of affection gripping his gut.

"You serious about this woman?"

Joe's stomach twisted. "Unfortunately."

Stan gave him a look of commiseration. "I'll tell you the truth. Jenna Jean is a high-maintenance woman. She doesn't take any bull and she demands the very best from me. But nobody has given me one-tenth of what she has given me. No woman has ever made the pieces of this planet snap together for me like she does. I knew that if I let her go, I would be losing the best thing that had ever come into my sorry life."

Joe felt the punch of Stan's every word. In his gut. In his heart. With every passing moment, he knew Marley was his destiny. He just didn't know how to make her believe it too. He rolled the bottle between his hands and eyed Stan with skepticism. "So, how did you get her? How did you keep her?"

"Three rules for getting her," Stan said, leaning forward on the table. "Persistence, persistence, persistence."

Stan's words reminded Joe of his own attitude

about getting into the Bad Boys' club. If he kept coming around, maybe they would let him stay. Eventually they had.

"And keeping her," Stan said with a wry chuckle, "will be the project of my life."

Marley dragged her luggage from the satellite parking van to her snow-covered car. She unlocked her car, thanked heaven it started with the first try, then left the engine running while she cleared the windshield. After the ride on the underground tram, the wait at baggage pickup, and the shuttle to her car, she felt as if she'd taken a major trek. And that was *after* she got off the airplane.

All the while, she thought of Joe.

Tense from traveling and trying to make sense of her feelings, Marley exited the parking lot and drove toward the toll booths. She needed to see Joe, to talk to him. The holidays had been difficult. Her traditional father couldn't comprehend why Marley refused to marry the father of her child, and her mother urged her to move back to Baltimore.

After that mind-blowing night she'd spent with Joe, she'd been frightened out of her wits by the power of her feelings for him. She had needed to clear her head. When the haze of fear had cleared, she hadn't liked what she'd learned.

She paid her parking fee, then joined the heavy, late-afternoon traffic on the interstate. She began to mentally rehearse what she wanted to say to Joe. *I love you, and I want to—*

A truck swerved into her lane. Marley slammed on her brakes, and the last thing she felt was the air bag hitting her face.

Joe's pager went off as he was driving home. He checked the unfamiliar number twice, and picked up his cell phone.

"Emergency Room, Denver General Hospital."

He tensed, his mind immediately shooting off in five different directions. "This is Joe Caruthers. I just received a page."

"Hold just a moment."

Joe frowned and turned off the interstate. His stomach began to churn. Marley was supposed to arrive back in town today. But the hospital wouldn't call him about her, he told himself. He wasn't her husband. Familiar frustration tugged at him, making him impatient.

"Mr. Caruthers, you are listed as the contact in case of emergency for Marley Fuller. Ms. Fuller has been in an accident and is being treated for injuries."

Joe's blood ran cold. "How bad is it?"

"I don't have that information. She..."

The woman's voice went on, but it was just noise to Joe. Senseless noise. *What if he lost her?* The possibility stopped his heart. After searching for her his entire life, he couldn't lose her.

He made a U-turn in the middle of the road and sped to the hospital. The drive was a blur. When he arrived, he pulled into a nonparking zone, not giving a rip if the Suburban got towed.

Pushing through the glass doors, he ran to the desk. "I'm here to see Marley Fuller."

A receptionist glanced at her chart. "She's conscious, now. We've taken her insurance information. You can—"

"Conscious *now*," he repeated, alarm rushing through him. "Where is she?"

As soon as the receptionist replied, Joe was moving toward Marley. He pulled back a curtain and found her in a bed with some kind of belt wrapped around her belly and her gaze fixed on a monitor on the table beside her. Her face was cut and bruised, and she was wiping tears from her face.

His heart twisted at the sight of her. "Marley," he said.

She jerked her head around to greet him. "Oh, Joe," she said and her face crumpled.

He rushed forward to hold her, but she squeezed his arms and gently pushed him away. "You can't hold me," she said in a voice tight with tears. "The baby's on a monitor, and we have to make sure everything is okay."

His throat tightened with dread. "Monitor?"

She closed her eyes and took a shaky breath. "Oh, God, you have no idea how much I wish you could hold me right now," she whispered, then took another breath. "This belt is an external monitor that measures the baby's heartbeat and my contractions. The baby's heartbeat is fine. I had a few contractions when I first arrived, but it looks like they've stopped."

"What happened?"

"I was in an accident on the interstate. A man pulled in front of me."

She looked so small and fragile in the hospital gown. It was torture not to be able to hold her tight. He swallowed over the wedge of alarm in his throat. "Where the hell is the doctor?" he demanded, rejecting the feeling of helplessness.

"The nurse will be back in a few minutes. She said it's just a matter of waiting right now," she said.

"Marley," he began.

She lifted her hand for him to stop. "No, I need to talk to you. I need to tell you that you were right. I was frightened because you're not safe. Being with you makes me feel out of control sometimes."

Her distress put a knot in his gut. "Marley," he said again.

"But being safe isn't always the best choice and—"

Joe couldn't hold it in any longer. "Marley, I love you, and I want you, even if something terrible happens to the baby. God knows I don't want it to. I want you as my wife, but I'll take you any way I can have you."

She stared at him, then squished her eyes closed, sending a stream of tears down her cheeks. "You *had* to tell me that when I can barely touch you."

He took both her hands in his, and she squeezed him so tightly she left nail prints on his skin. "Tell you what?"

"That you love me. You've never said it before."

Joe swallowed his regret. "I fought it. It took me a while to figure out I didn't have a tin heart after all. I don't want to lose you."

Sniffing, she opened her eyes and shook her head. "That won't happen. What I was trying to tell you was that I feel more alive with you than I've ever felt. Being with you is like seeing all the colors of the rainbow, when I saw only a few of them before. I love you so much—" she faltered and blinked back fresh tears "—so much it scares me sometimes."

His chest ached with the power of his feelings for her. "Say you'll marry me, Marley."

"Oh, yes," she whispered, and gave a watery smile that reminded him of the sun trying to push through a rain cloud. "Instead of an engagement ring, would you please get me a Sherman tank to drive?"

Hours later, when the doctor released Marley, Joe took her home and carried her up the stairs. Although she still felt a little shaky from the accident, she chided him. "This is not necessary."

"Tough," he said, carefully setting her down on the bed. "I want you to stay here and not move."

"For how long?"

"A long time," he told her, stripping off his clothes.

"A long time?" she asked, suspecting he had something ridiculous in mind. "Are we talking four hours or four months."

"Four months is a good start," he said, joining her on the bed.

"Well I might have to use the bathroom some-time," she reminded him.

Joe shook his head. "Nope. You'll just have to hold it."

She laughed. "You're crazy!"

"We're not discussing my sanity right now, since you're responsible for my loss of it," he told her, and brushed her forehead with a gentle kiss. "We're discussing where you're going to plant yourself. I want you to stay right there, so I'll know you're safe. I want you to stay right there and never, ever leave."

Marley saw that her coming and going had wounded him, and her heart hurt at the realization. She lifted her hand to his chest and felt the solid beat of his heart against her palm. "I'm not going any-where," she told him. "I'm staying here with you."

"Good," he said, pulling her down with him. "I'm glad we don't have to argue."

"No arguments on this," she told him and smiled. "I love you."

Joe met her gaze with a solemn expression on his face. "I love you."

Marley slept late, and by midday, there was a new Volvo in the driveway. She didn't quarrel over the car, and didn't question him when he immediately arranged to have her belongings moved to his house. She understood the intensity of his need for her, be-cause it was completely reciprocal. Marley also knew, however, that her life with Joe would be filled to the gills with negotiations, and not all of them would be peaceable. When she finally talked Joe into letting her out of the house three days later, he took her to a jewelry store, and she could envision World War III starting in Denver, Colorado.

Marley tried to be gentle by telling Joe she wasn't comfortable wearing such a large stone, but after the third attempt, she was forced to take off the gloves. "It's obscene. I won't wear it," she told him firmly.

"It's one of those things that will just take a little getting used to," he said, reaching for her hand.

She pulled her hand away from him. "I'll need a crane to lift my hand."

"Then I'll buy a damn crane."

The jeweler looked back and forth between the two of them as if he were watching a Ping-Pong game.

"Would you like to tattoo your name on my forehead?" Marley asked, losing her patience.

"Don't tempt me," he muttered.

She took a deep breath and counted to ten. She couldn't fault him so much for his possessiveness, because she felt the same way about him. Her colleagues would use the nice civilized term of mutual exclusivity. Marley's feelings for Joe were more primitive. He belonged to her, and she belonged to him.

She took his hand in hers. "Honey, I don't want an engagement ring. I would rather have a pretty wedding band with my birthstones and diamonds."

He stared at her a moment in surprise.

The jeweler cleared his throat. "May I make a few suggestions?"

Joe nodded. "Go ahead."

Marley selected three different rings she favored. "I'd like you to surprise me with the final choice," she said. "While we're here, we can look at rings for you."

He looked taken aback. "For me?"

She pulled him closer and kissed him right there in the middle of the jewelry store. "Either that or I suppose you could get my name tattooed on your forehead."

Epilogue

He would have showered her with fine jewels, but she had refused. "If you're going to spoil me, spoil me with you," she'd said.

He would have given her the world, but she'd beat him to the punch and given it to him.

Joe was literally holding the world in his arms on this fine July morning. The view of the Rocky Mountains was breathtaking, but it couldn't command his attention. On his rooftop balcony, Marley shared the chaise longue with him, leaning against his chest as she cradled their son in her arms.

Just out of bed, he'd pulled on a pair of jeans, and she wore a white nightgown he'd discarded the night before. He glanced down at her toes peeking from beneath the hem and felt that same tingle in his hand again. Sometimes he still couldn't believe he'd found her.

"He's going to break hearts," Marley said, looking down at their three-month-old son. "He looks just like you."

Joe grinned and toyed with her hair. "I wonder if there's some kind of liability insurance a parent can buy for a kid who breaks hearts instead of windows," he ventured.

Marley rolled her eyes at him. "Will you look into that before you get his first car, or will you start his IRA first?"

Joe winced. "His first car."

They looked at each other, then said in unison, "A tank."

Marley laughed lightly, then sobered and lifted her fingers to his lips. "How do you feel about having a son?"

His chest tightened with pride and love as he looked down at his son's face. "There aren't words. I want to give him everything. I want to give you both everything."

Marley shook her head, and her heart was in her eyes. "We don't want everything. We want you." She smiled. "Although, if we ever move from this house, would you build me a tree house?"

Joe chuckled. "Sure, but you would have to learn the secret password in order to get in."

Her gaze turned sexy. "How much persuasion would it take for you to tell me the secret password?"

Joe felt the familiar surge of need in his blood, in

his heart. He lowered his mouth to hers. "Continuous persuasion. That's part of the secret. You can't ever stop."

"I won't," she said, sighing in pleasure. "Did you ever dream it could be this good?"

"Marley, I never had dreams this good."

* * * * *

Take 2 bestselling love stories FREE

Plus get a FREE surprise gift!

Special Limited-Time Offer

Mail to Silhouette Reader Service™

3010 Walden Avenue
P.O. Box 1867
Buffalo, N.Y. 14240-1867

YES! Please send me 2 free Silhouette Desire® novels and my free surprise gift. Then send me 6 brand-new novels every month, which I will receive months before they appear in bookstores. Bill me at the low price of $3.12 each plus 25¢ delivery and applicable sales tax, if any.* That's the complete price, and a saving of over 10% off the cover prices—quite a bargain! I understand that accepting the books and gift places me under no obligation ever to buy any books. I can always return a shipment and cancel at any time. Even if I never buy another book from Silhouette, the 2 free books and the surprise gift are mine to keep forever.

225 SEN CH7U

Name		(PLEASE PRINT)	
Address		Apt. No.	
City		State	Zip

This offer is limited to one order per household and not valid to present Silhouette Desire® subscribers. *Terms and prices are subject to change without notice.
Sales tax applicable in N.Y.

UDES-98

©1990 Harlequin Enterprises Limited

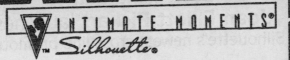

**Coming in October from
Silhouette Intimate Moments...**

BRIDES OF THE NIGHT

Silhouette Intimate Moments fulfills your wildest
wishes in this compelling new in-line collection
featuring two very memorable men...tantalizing,
irresistible men who exist only in the darkness
but who hunger for the light of true love.

TWILIGHT VOWS
by Maggie Shayne

The unforgettable WINGS IN THE NIGHT miniseries
continues with a vampire hero to die for and the
lovely mortal woman who will go to any lengths to
save their unexpected love.

MARRIED BY DAWN
by Marilyn Tracy

Twelve hours was all the time this rogue vampire
had to protect an innocent woman. But was
marriage his only choice to keep her safe—if not
from the night...then from himself?

*Look for BRIDES OF THE NIGHT this October,
wherever Silhouette books are sold.*

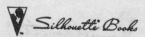

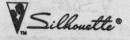

COMING NEXT MONTH

#1171 THE LIONESS TAMER—Rebecca Brandewyne

Corporate tycoon Jordan Westcott, October's *Man of the Month,* gave up his reign as King of the Cement Jungle for a *real* challenge—taming the virginal spitfire Mistral St. Michel. But once this magnificent stranger transformed Mistral's fierce roar into a velvet purr would he find *himself* coming out of the wilderness…and spending a lifetime in this lioness's den?

#1172 THE LONE RIDER TAKES A BRIDE—Leanne Banks
The Rulebreakers

Rebellious Ben Palmer traveled through life fast and *alone.* So he'd certainly never get involved with adventureless Amelia Russell. What would Miss Straight and Narrow do with windblown hair, skirt flying up above her knees, traveling by the light of the full midnight moon? Well, it might just be worth a spin around the block to find out….

#1173 THE PATERNITY FACTOR—Caroline Cross

Wide-eyed beauty Jessy Ross had secretly loved the intense and sexy Shane Wyatt for years. Now she was sharing his home and caring for his baby—*a baby he'd discovered wasn't his.* He had vowed never to trust another woman as long as he lived. But Jessy had made her *own* solemn promise. To get to the bottom of Shane's bitterness—then get her man.

#1174 THE NON-COMMISSIONED BABY—Maureen Child
The Bachelor Battalion

Assignment: Fatherhood. Captain Jeff Ryan had just landed his toughest duty ever—daddy to a six-month-old baby girl. The valiant soldier enlisted expert help in the form of Laura Morgan…and *her* lovely form could stop a battleship. But could it anchor the heart of one tough marine?

#1175 THE OUTLAW'S WIFE—Cindy Gerard
Outlaw Hearts

Headstrong Emma James was tired of playing happy little homemaker to a "disinterested" husband. But the last thing Garrett wanted to lose was his beloved wife. So, even if it meant tying her up and toting her off, he'd show his feisty wife exactly how he felt about her—outlaw style!

#1176 COWBOYS, BABIES AND SHOTGUN VOWS—Shirley Rogers
Women To Watch

No woman had ever walked out on Ryder McCall! Outrage sent the proud cowboy chasing after one-night lover Ashley Bennett—but he wasn't expecting that *she'd* be expecting. Ryder wanted to be a real father—*and* husband. Could he convert Ashley's flat "no way" to a willing "I do"?